"You like telling me what to do. Is this a military thing or a male thing?"

"I'm just trying to do the right thing," Jeff replied. "I need a housekeeper and you need to make a change in your life."

Ashley sighed. "It's not that I don't appreciate the offer, Jeff."

"But you don't trust me."

Her gaze sharpened. "It's not that exactly."

I want you.

The words remained unspoken, but they burned inside of him. He wanted to inhale the scent of her body, touch her everywhere. He wanted to fill her until they both forgot everything but the heat of the moment.

He drew in a slow breath. "The offer still stands. Let me know if you change your mind."

And then he walked away, because if he didn't, he might just tell her the truth.

That when he was with her and her daughter, he forgot he wasn't like everyone else.

Dear Reader,

Many people read romance novels for the unforgettable heroes that capture our hearts and stay with us long after the last page is read. But to give all the credit for the success of this genre to these handsome hunks is to underestimate the value of the heart of a romance: the heroine.

"Heroes are fantasy material, but for me, the heroines are much more grounded in real life," says Susan Mallery, bestselling author of this month's *Shelter in a Soldier's Arms*. "For me, the heroine is at the center of the story. I want to write and read about women who are intelligent, funny and determined."

Gina Wilkins's *The Stranger in Room 205* features a beautiful newspaper proprietor who discovers an amnesiac in her backyard and finds herself in an adventure of a lifetime! And don't miss *The M.D. Meets His Match* in Hades, Alaska, where Marie Ferrarella's snowbound heroine unexpectedly finds romance that is sure to heat up the bitter cold....

Peggy Webb delivers an *Invitation to a Wedding;* when the heroine is rescued from marrying the wrong man, could a long-lost friend end up being Mr. Right? Sparks fly in Lisette Belisle's novel when the heroine, raising *Her Sister's Secret Son,* meets a mysterious man who claims to be the boy's father! And in Patricia McLinn's *Almost a Bride,* a rancher desperate to save her ranch enters into a marriage of convenience, but with temptation as her bed partner, life becomes a minefield of desire.

Special Edition is proud to publish novels featuring strong, admirable heroines struggling to balance life, love and family and making dreams come true. Enjoy! And look inside for details about our Silhouette Makes You a Star contest.

Best,

Karen Taylor Richman, Senior Editor

Please address questions and book requests to:
Silhouette Reader Service
U.S.: 3010 Walden Ave., P.O. Box 1325, Buffalo, NY 14269
Canadian: P.O. Box 609, Fort Erie, Ont. L2A 5X3

Shelter in a Soldier's Arms

SUSAN MALLERY

SPECIAL EDITION™

Published by Silhouette Books

America's Publisher of Contemporary Romance

To single mothers everywhere. May your dedication be
rewarded with love, happiness and your heart's desire.

 SILHOUETTE BOOKS

ISBN 0-373-24400-2

SHELTER IN A SOLDIER'S ARMS

Copyright © 2001 by Susan Macias-Redmond

Visit Silhouette at www.eHarlequin.com

Printed in U.S.A.

Books by Susan Mallery

SUSAN MALLERY

is the bestselling author of over forty books for Harlequin and Silhouette. She makes her home in the Pacific Northwest with her handsome prince of a husband and her two adorable-but-not-bright cats.

Dear Reader,

I was so excited to find out that my book was going to be part of Special Edition's new promotion, A WOMAN'S WAY. While I frequently write stories about strong women who find an extraordinary love, I felt that this particular heroine deserved special notice.

Ashley Churchill is like so many of us—trapped in circumstances she can't quite control. She's a struggling single mom trying to get her degree. Money is tight, time is tighter. Yet she has a terrific relationship with her daughter and she has a plan. With love and a plan, a woman can do almost anything.

When Jeff Ritter sweeps into her life, she's not sure if she's being rescued or taken hostage. Jeff is every inch a soldier—he's lost the tenderness in his heart, if he ever had any. Yet he is the most honorable man she's ever known…and the sexiest. He frightens her, because a man who has nothing to lose is a dangerous creature. Yet he is both kind to her and her daughter—and incredibly handsome. She can't resist him, even when she knows she's crazy to let herself fall for him.

I hope you enjoy this passionate story.

All the best,

Susan Mallery

Chapter One

There was trouble.

Jeffrey Ritter sensed it even before he spotted the flashing light on the security console mounted in his car. At five o'clock in the morning the offices of Ritter/Rankin Security should have been locked down and empty. According to the red flashing light, the building was neither.

Jeff touched several buttons on the console to confirm the information. The front and rear doors were locked, but inner doors were open. Lights were on as well, he noted as he drove into the parking lot and headed for a spot to the left of the double glass doors—glass that was deceptively clear but could in fact withstand severe artillery fire and a small bomb blast.

Trouble, he thought again as he put the car into

Park and turned off the engine. He popped the trunk of his black BMW 740i and stepped out onto the damp pavement. Although it wasn't raining, the air was heavy and wet, as if the Seattle skies were about to do their thing at any moment.

Jeff circled the vehicle and removed his personal firearm, which he checked and slipped into his specially designed holster. Next came the black stunner, designed to immobilize an attacker without permanent injury. He punched buttons on his beeper, setting it to standby so that a single touch would alert his partner and the authorities. He didn't usually get the latter involved in his operations, but his office was in downtown Seattle. The local police wouldn't appreciate a predawn shoot-out, and they would absolutely expect an explanation.

He turned his attention to the quiet building. Nothing looked out of place. But in his experience that was common. Danger rarely announced itself with a neon sign.

Jeff walked quickly and quietly, moving around the building to a side entrance without a lock. Only a small keypad allowed access. He tapped in the code and waited for the door to unlock. If someone was waiting in the small alcove, the door wouldn't open. There was a slight *snick* as the locking mechanism released, and he entered the protective space tucked along the main corridor.

He was surrounded on three sides by glass coated to be a two-way mirror. Dropping into a crouch, he surveyed the length of the corridor. Nothing. From the corner of his eye he caught a flicker of movement in the east hallway. It was gone before he could register who or what it was. Damn.

Still crouching, Jeff pushed the concealed button to let himself out into the corridor. He hurried in the direction of the movement, keeping low, running soundlessly. As he rounded the corner, he reached for both the gun and the stunner—only to slam to a halt, as immobilized as if he'd just taken a jolt from his own weapon.

Breath left his lungs. Involuntary impulses forced him to his feet even as he slipped the weapons out of sight. He didn't remember making a sound, yet he must have because the intruder turned and looked at him.

"You hafta be quiet 'cause Mommy's sleeping."

In less than a second he'd scanned the immediate area and absorbed all that he saw. No dangerous intruders, at least not in the traditional sense. Which was unfortunate. Jeff Ritter knew what to do when facing an insurrection, a terrorist hit squad or even a stubborn client. But he had absolutely no experience with children—especially little girls with big blue eyes.

She was small, barely coming to midthigh on him. Dark, shiny curls caught the overhead light. She wore pink kitten-motif pajamas and fluffy, cotton-candy-colored slippers. A stuffed white cat filled her arms.

He blinked, half wondering if she was an illusion. But she remained stubbornly real. As did the woman on the floor beside her.

Jeff took in the cart of cleaning supplies and the woman's casual, worn clothes. Grown-ups he could handle, and he quickly cataloged her flushed face, closed eyes and the trace of sweat on her forehead. Even from several feet away he could sense her fever, brought on by illness. She'd probably sat down to rest and had slipped into semi-consciousness.

"Mommy works hard," the little girl told him. "She's real tired. I woke up a while ago and I was gonna talk to her 'bout why she was sleeping on the floor, but then I thought I'd be real quiet and let her sleep."

Chubby cheeks tilted up as the young child smiled at him, as if expecting praise for her decision. Instead Jeff turned his pager from emergency stand-by to regular, then flicked on the safety on his gun and switched off the stunner. Then he crouched next to the woman.

"What's your name?"

He was speaking to the adult, but the child answered instead.

"I'm Maggie. Do you work here? It's nice. One of the big rooms is my favorite. It's got really, really big windows and you can see forever, clear up to the sky. Sometimes when I wakes up, I count the stars. I can count to a hundred and sometimes I can count higher. Wanna hear?"

"Not right now."

Jeff ignored the ongoing chatter. Instead he reached for the woman's forehead and at the same time he touched the inside of her wrist to check her pulse. Her heart rate was steady and strong, but she definitely had a fever. He reached to lift an eyelid to examine her pupil reaction when she awakened. Her eyes fluttered open and she stared at him, her expression telling him he was about as welcome as the plague.

A man! Ashley Churchill's first thought was that Damian had come back to haunt her. Her second was that while the cold-looking man in front of her might be second cousin to the devil, he wasn't her ex-husband.

Her head felt as if it weighed three tons, and she couldn't seem to focus on anything but gray eyes and a face completely devoid of emotion. Then she blinked and brain cells began firing, albeit slowly. She was sitting in a hallway that looked vaguely familiar. Ritter/Rankin Security, she thought hazily. She was working, or at least she was supposed to be.

"I was so tired," she murmured, trying to sound more coherent than she felt. "I sat down to rest. I guess I fell asleep." She blinked again, then wished she hadn't as she recognized the man crouched in front of her. He'd passed her in the hall when she first interviewed for the job. The office manager had identified him as Jeffrey Ritter, partner, professional security expert extraordinaire, ex-soldier.

Her boss.

"Mommy, you're awake!"

The familiar voice normally made her heart leap with gladness, but now Ashley felt only horror. Maggie was up? What time...? She glanced at her watch and groaned when she saw 5:10 a.m. glowing in the light of the hall. She was supposed to have finished her cleaning by two, and she always met the deadline. She remembered something about security systems reactivating after she'd left.

"I'm sorry, Mr. Ritter," she said, forcing herself

to scramble to her feet and ignoring the weakness that filled her when she did. "I don't usually sleep on the job. Maggie had the flu last week and I think I caught her bug." In fact, she was sure of it. Not that the stern, unsmiling man standing in front of her would care one way or the other.

He turned his attention from her to her daughter. Ashley winced, knowing it looked bad. No one had ever explicitly said she couldn't bring her daughter to work, but then no doubt no one had thought they would have to. Four-year-olds didn't belong in the workplace.

"Mommy says preschool is a germ mag-mag-maggot?" Her rosebud mouth couldn't quite get around the word.

"Magnet," Ashley offered automatically. She smoothed her hands against her jeans and offered her hand to the man who was very likely going to fire her. "Mr. Ritter, I'm Ashley Churchill. Obviously I clean the office. Usually I'm out by two."

"I sleep while Mommy works," Maggie put in helpfully. "Mommy makes me a really nice bed with my favorite kitten sheets. She sings to me and I close my eyes." She lowered her voice and took a step toward the man. "I'm s'posed to go right to sleep but sometimes I peek and look at the stars."

Ashley swallowed against the lump of fear in her throat. "Yes, well, it's not as bad as it seems," she said lamely, knowing it was actually worse. She felt slightly less perky than a fur ball and she was going to lose her job. Talk about a lousy start to her day. At least things could only get better from here.

"Your things are in my office?"

Jeff Ritter spoke for the first time. His voice was low and perfectly modulated. She had no clue what he was thinking, which made her assume the worst.

"Ah, yes."

"Where do the cleaning supplies go?" he asked.

"There's a closet at the end of the hall. I'd nearly finished. I still have to take care of Mr. Rankin's office. Everything else is done."

He took her elbow and led her down the hall. His touch was steel. Not especially rough or firm, but she knew that if she tried to escape he could snap her in half. Like a toothpick.

A charming visual, she thought with a sigh. Her daughter could collect the splintered shards of what used to be her mother and keep them in a little box. She could bring her out at show-and-tell when she went to school and—

Ashley shook her head. She was sicker than she'd thought. Her mind was wandering and she would give almost anything to be in her bed and have this all be a horrible dream. But it wasn't. As they stepped into Jeff's office, the proof of her audacious behavior lay scattered all around.

One of the plush leather sofas had been made up into a bed. There were a half-dozen stuffed animals scattered across the kitten sheets. A juice box and crumbs were testament to a late-night snack, while a baby monitor held the place of honor in the center of the large glass coffee table she'd pushed away from the sofa.

He released her and crossed to the table. When he picked up the monitor, Ashley reached into her pocket and removed the small receiver.

"It's so I can hear her," she said, probably unnecessarily. The man was a security expert. He would have access to listening devices she could only imagine. "I don't bring Maggie to work with me on a whim, Mr. Ritter. I go to college during the day, which is why I work the hours I do. I can't afford to pay someone to spend the night. A sitter would take most of my paycheck and I need that for rent, food and tuition."

She briefly closed her eyes as the room began to spin. He wouldn't care, she thought glumly. He was going to fire her. She would lose both her paycheck and her health insurance. Still, she wouldn't go without a fight.

"She's never been any trouble. It's been nearly a year and no one has ever found out." She winced at how that sounded. "I'm not saying that to excuse my behavior, just to point out that she's not really a problem." *She's not a reason to fire me.* Except she didn't say that.

Maggie moved to her side and took her hand. "Don't worry, Mommy. The nice man likes us."

Oh, yeah, Ashley thought. Maybe served up for breakfast, but not any other way. There was something scary about the man in front of her. Something she couldn't exactly put her finger on. A stillness, maybe? Or maybe it was his eyes—so cold. He studied her like a predator assessing a potential victim.

Jeff Ritter was tall, maybe six-two or three. His tailored suit looked expensive and well cut, but it couldn't conceal the power of his body. He was a honed fighting machine. Maybe a killing one.

He was blond, with eyes the color of slate. In another life he could have been described as handsome, but not in this one. There was too much wariness in his stance, too much danger.

Because of the hours she worked, she didn't have contact with very many people in the office. Once every three weeks she checked in with the office manager. Instructions were left on the bulletin board in the supply closet, her paychecks were mailed to her house. But she'd read articles about the security firm. There had been several write-ups when a computer expert's son had been kidnapped and held for ransom. Jeff had been the one to track down the criminals. He'd brought them back, more dead than alive. The boy had been fine.

A shiver rippled through her. It had nothing to do with fear and everything to do with the fever heating her system. Her stomach lurched and she knew if she'd eaten dinner, she would have just shared it with the world.

Jeff gave her a quick once-over then moved to the sofa. "You're ready to pass out on your feet. You need to be home and in bed."

Before she could protest, he'd gathered the sheets and stuffed them into the tote on the floor by the sofa. Maggie joined in the game, collecting her stuffed animals. While she carefully threw out the empty juice container, Jeff put the baby monitor into the bag.

"Anything else?" he asked.

Just her final paycheck, she thought grimly. But that would be sent to her.

"Nothing. Thank you, Mr. Ritter. You've been very kind."

She didn't know what else to say. Would he respond to begging? Based on the chill in his gray eyes, she didn't think so.

He didn't acknowledge her words. Instead he turned and headed for the front of the building.

"My car's out back," she called after him, then had to lean against the door frame to gather her strength. She needed to sleep. Unfortunately Maggie wasn't going to go down for more than a couple of hours. Maybe that would be enough to get Ashley on her feet enough to get through the day. Or maybe—

"You're too ill to drive," Jeff said flatly. He'd paused at the turn in the corridor. "I'll take you home. Your car will be returned to you later in the day."

She was too weak to argue, which meant he was right about her being in no shape to drive. Slowly she staggered after him. Maggie held her hand.

"Snowball says she wants to sleep with you when we get home," Maggie said sleepily as they walked through the building. "She's magic and she'll make you feel better."

Ashley knew that her daughter wouldn't give up her favorite toy lightly. Touched by the gesture, she smiled at her child. "I think you're the magic one."

Maggie giggled, her curls dancing. "I'm just little, Mommy. There's no place for the magic to go. If I was bigger, there could be some."

Ashley was too tired to point out that Snowball was smaller still. But then, favorite toys were always special in ways that grown-ups didn't understand.

They stepped out into the misting morning to find Jeff holding open the rear door of an impressive black sedan. Ashley didn't have to see the BMW emblem on the hood to know that the car was expensive. Very expensive. If she could make even close to what this car cost, all her troubles would be solved.

She hesitated before sliding across the soft, gray leather. It was cool and smooth and soft. *Whatever you do, don't throw up,* she told herself firmly.

It took only a few seconds to secure her daughter and herself in safety belts. With her arm around Maggie, Ashley leaned back and closed her eyes. Just a few more minutes, she told herself. Fifteen at most. Then she would be home and crawling into her own bed.

"I need your address."

The voice came out of the blackness. Ashley had to rouse herself to speak and even then it was difficult to form words. She started to give him directions, as well, but Jeff informed her he knew the area. She didn't doubt him. He was the kind of man who knew just about everything.

The soft hum of the engine lulled her into that half-awake, half-asleep place. She could have stayed there forever. The early hour caught up with Maggie who snuggled against her and relaxed. Right up until the car came to a stop and she felt more than heard Jeff turn toward her.

"There seems to be a problem."

Ashley forced her eyes open, then wished she hadn't. So much for her day not getting worse.

They were stopped close to her four-story apartment building. Normally there was plenty of room to park right in front of the building, but not this morning. Today, red fire trucks and police cars had pulled into the driveway. Flashing lights twinkled in the light rainfall. Stunned, Ashley stared in disbelief at the river of water flowing down the main steps. Her neighbors were huddled together on the sidewalk.

No, she thought, feeling herself tremble with shock and disbelief. This couldn't be happening. Not today.

She fumbled with Maggie's seat belt, then her own. After opening the rear door, she stepped out, pulling her daughter with her. She was careful to hold Maggie in her arms. The girl's slippers wouldn't provide any protection against the water flowing everywhere.

"Mommy, what happened?" Maggie asked.

"I don't know."

Mrs. Gunther, the retired, blue-haired woman who managed the aging apartment building, spotted her and hurried over.

"Ashley, you're not going to believe it. The main water pipe broke about an hour ago. It's a mess. From what I've learned, it will take a week to repair the damage. They'll escort you inside to get whatever you can carry out, then we have to make other arrangements until the pipe is repaired."

Jeff watched the last trace of color drain from the woman's face. Defeat clouded her eyes, making her tremble. Or maybe it was the fever.

"I don't have anywhere to go," she whispered.

The old lady patted her arm. "I'm in the same situation, dear. Not to worry. They're opening a shelter. We'll be fine there."

Maggie, the moppet with dark curls and a far-too-trusting smile, looked at her mother. "What's a shelter, Mommy? Do they got kittens there? Real ones?"

"I—I don't know."

Ashley shifted her daughter's weight, then stared

at the gushing building. "I need to get my textbooks and notes. Clothes for us, some toys."

"They'll escort you in," the old woman said. "I'll watch Maggie while you're there."

Suddenly Ashley seemed to remember him. She turned and blinked. "Oh, Mr. Ritter. Thanks for the ride. I, um, guess I need to get my things out of your trunk."

She moved to the rear of the vehicle and waited until he'd popped open the trunk. When she swung the tote bag onto her shoulder, she had to take a quick step to steady herself.

"Are you going to be all right?"

The question surprised them both. Jeff hadn't planned to ask it. He told himself that her situation wasn't his problem. The woman would be fine in a shelter. His gaze drifted to the little girl all in pink. He was less sure about her doing well under those circumstances.

"We'll be great." Ashley gave him a false smile. "You've been too kind already."

It was his cue to leave. Normally he would have melted into the crowd and been gone before anyone knew he was even there. Instead he lingered.

"You can't take her there," he said, his voice low and urgent. "It's not right."

"She'll be fine," Ashley assured him. "We'll be fine together."

He told himself to step back, to not get involved. He told himself— "I'll pay for a hotel room if you'd like."

Her eyes were an odd hazel color. Neither blue nor

green. Not brown. Some swirling combination of all the colors.

"You've been very kind already. Goodbye, Mr. Ritter."

She dismissed him. He accepted her decision, but before she took a step away, he slipped one of his business cards into her jacket pocket. It was an impulsive act, so unlike him. Later he would try to figure out why he'd bothered. Then he did what he was good at. He blended in, moving toward his car. In a matter of seconds, he was gone.

"You plan on joining the conversation anytime soon?"

Jeff looked at his friend and partner, Zane Rankin, and shrugged. "I'm here."

"Physically. But you keep drifting off. Not like you at all."

Jeff returned his attention to the plans on the table without acknowledging the truth of Zane's words. Jeff *was* having trouble concentrating on the work at hand. He knew the cause—he couldn't get the woman and her child out of his head and he didn't know why.

Was it their circumstances? Yet he'd seen hundreds in worse trouble. Compared to a war-torn village with its winter food stores destroyed, Ashley Churchill's plight was insignificant. Was it the child? The girl? Maggie's bright smile, her foolish trust, her pink pajamas and stuffed, white cat were so far from his world as to belong to a distant universe.

Did it matter why they haunted him? Better the living than the dead who were his usual companions.

There were no answers to any of the questions, so

he dismissed them and returned his attention to the diagram of a luxury villa overlooking the Mediterranean. The private residence was to host a secret gathering of several international business executives who were responsible for the manufacture of some of the world's most deadly weapons. The threat of industrial espionage, terrorist attack or kidnapping would be high. He and Zane were to provide the security. Step one: learn the weaknesses of the location.

Jeff pointed with his pen. ''All this has to go,'' he said, indicating a lush tropical garden creeping down a hill.

''Agreed. We'll use the latest class-ten sensors, hiding them on what's left.''

The new high-tech sensors could be programmed to ignore the movement of the security team, yet pick up the wanderings of a field mouse at fifty yards.

''What about—''

The buzz of his intercom interrupted him. Jeff frowned. His assistant, Brenda, knew better than to bother him and Zane while they were involved in tactical planning. She would only do so if there was an emergency.

''Yes,'' he said, as he tapped a button on his phone.

''Jeff, I know you're busy but you have a call from a downtown shelter. About a Ms. Churchill and her daughter. I didn't know...'' His normally take-charge assistant sounded fairly flustered. ''Is she a friend of yours? Or should I take a message?''

All of his senses went on alert. ''Put the call through,'' he instructed.

There was a moment of silence, followed by

Brenda's voice politely saying, "Mr. Ritter is on the phone now."

"This is Jeff Ritter. How can I help you?"

"Oh, Mr. Ritter. Hi. I'm Julie, a volunteer at the shelter. Ashley and Maggie Churchill are here. The problem is Ashley is very sick. Too sick to stay, but she's refusing to go to a hospital. As she only seems to have the flu, I can't blame her. But we don't have the facilities to take care of her. We found your card in her jacket pocket and I was wondering if you're a friend of the family."

Jeff knew what she was asking. Would he take responsibility? He reminded himself that Ashley Churchill had already refused his offer to pay for a hotel. Then he remembered the defeat in her eyes when she'd seen the ruin that was her home. She was sick, she had a child and nowhere to go.

It wasn't his problem, he reminded himself. He didn't get involved. Not ever. According to his ex-wife he had the compassion of the devil himself and a heart made of stone. Telling the shelter volunteer he wasn't anything to the Churchill females was the only thing that made sense.

"Yes, I'm a friend of the family," he said instead. "I'll be right there to pick them both up. They can stay with me."

Chapter Two

Ashley tried to remember when she last felt this horrible. It wasn't just her unsettled stomach, the pounding in her head or even the weakness that invaded her body. She'd reached the absolute low point of her life. In one morning she'd lost her job and her home, and now she and her daughter were being thrown out of the temporary shelter. In her head she knew that it was wrong of her to stay and expose everyone to the flu. There were several elderly residents, along with mothers with babies. But in her heart she felt incredibly alone. Where were she and Maggie supposed to go? She didn't have the money for a hotel, and even if she did, Ashley knew she was close to physical collapse. If—or rather when—that happened, who was going to watch over her daughter?

Involuntarily her eyelids closed. She desperately

wanted to sleep. She wanted this horrible nightmare to end. And just once in her life, she wanted someone else to take charge and make everything better. She wanted to be rescued, just like in those fairy tales she read to her daughter. However, it seemed unlikely a handsome prince would show up to take her away from all her troubles and…

A shadow fell across the cot. Even with her eyes closed Ashley noted the sudden darkening. She forced herself to gather her last bit of strength and look at her visitor. Probably the shelter volunteer, Julie something, who had gently explained she couldn't stay.

But the person looming over her wasn't a too-perky student from the nearby college. Rather he was tall, silent and frighteningly familiar. Not a handsome prince, but the evil wizard—a creature both powerful and deadly.

She knew she was hallucinating, because there was no way her soon-to-be ex-boss was really gathering her up in his arms. She was still lying on the cot, imagining it, she told herself even as powerful male strength surrounded her. The illusion was surprisingly real and in it, he carried her as easily as she carried Maggie.

"You're staying with me until you're better," Jeff Ritter said.

She blinked. The voice sounded genuine and she felt the soft whisper of his breath across her cheek as he spoke. Now that she made herself think about it, she could feel the smooth wool of his suit where her hand rested just below his collar at the back of his neck. She blinked, not sure what was real and what was fever induced.

"Are you carrying me?"

Gray eyes stared into her face. "You're sicker than I thought."

True or not, it wasn't much of an answer.

"We can't—" She pressed her lips together. What couldn't they do? She couldn't remember.

"You'll be safe at my house," he told her.

Safe? Not likely. Suddenly she was being lowered into nothing. She clutched at Jeff, then sighed in relief when he settled her onto a chair.

"Collect her things," he said to someone just out of Ashley's field of vision.

"I'll get her shoes."

The last statement, spoken in her daughter's bright, cheerful voice, brought Ashley back to the land of the living faster than any drug.

"Maggie?"

"She'll be fine."

She shook her head slightly and ignored the subsequent wooziness. With a couple of deep breaths, she managed to clear her head enough to focus on the man crouched in front of her. She hadn't been mistaken—it was Jeff Ritter, all right. Still dressed in his well-tailored suit, still looking distant and the tiniest bit scary.

"Why are you here?" she asked.

"Because you're too sick to stay at the shelter. I'm taking you home until you're on your feet."

She wiggled her sock-clad toes and wondered if he had any idea that she felt as if she was going to be sick forever.

"We can't," she told him. "I mean, we don't even know you."

His steel-gray eyes stared directly into hers. She searched for some flicker of warmth, of humanity, but there was nothing but her tiny reflection in his irises.

"What do you want to know?" he asked. "Should I give you a list of references?"

That would be a start, she thought, but didn't dare speak the words.

Surprisingly Jeff reached out and touched her cheek with his fingers. Just a fleeting moment of contact, during which she felt heat and amazing gentleness.

"Don't be afraid," he said quietly. "I'm not going to hurt you or Maggie. You're sick. You need a place to stay. I'm offering one. End of story. I won't hurt you or pressure you."

"But..."

"You have anywhere else to go?" he asked.

She shook her head. She wished the answer were different, but it wasn't. Her solitary job meant she didn't have any work friends, and she was always rushing into class from dropping Maggie off at school or hurrying out of class to pick up her daughter, so she'd never had time to make friends at the university. Her only acquaintances were her neighbors who were in the same situation she was.

"Mommy, here are your shoes."

She was more awake now and could offer her daughter a hug and her thanks when the happy little girl returned with her athletic shoes.

Before she could bend over and loosen the laces, Jeff took them from her and began slipping the right shoe on her foot.

The touch of his hand on her ankle was surprisingly

intimate. She felt embarrassed and light-headed. The latter sensation could have been from the fever she was fighting, but she didn't think so. Still, it was equally unlikely it was because of what Jeff was doing. He was being kind, nothing more. He was a stranger. A slightly scary stranger. She thought of him as an ice-cold killer, not an attractive man.

"Mommy helps me with my shoes, too," Maggie offered, leaning against Ashley. "With my pink shoes, she has to tie the bow two times instead of just one, 'cause they're so long." Her voice indicated her reverence at the additional work her mother was willing to perform.

"I think I can get by with just one bow," Jeff said, as he finished with the first shoe and started on the second. "Are you ready to go?"

"I need a coat," the girl informed him.

"Do you know where yours is?"

Maggie nodded, then took off in the direction of their cot. Ashley waited until Jeff finished with her shoes and straightened.

The room wasn't spinning so much now and her head felt slightly more clear than when she'd first awakened. Her body still ached and she knew she looked horrible, but as long as her brain continued to function, they would be fine.

"You're acting as if it's all decided," she said.

"Isn't it?" He jerked his head toward the cot where two members of the volunteer staff were already collecting her things. "You need time and a place to recover. I can provide both."

"I want to trust you. As you've already learned,

I'm running out of options. But I still have questions. I don't know why you're doing this.''

For the first time since he arrived, he wouldn't meet her gaze. He looked over her head, but she doubted he was seeing the bustling activities in the temporary shelter. He'd gone somewhere else, and based on what she knew about it, it wasn't a place she wanted to know about.

Finally he shrugged. ''I'm under my good-deed quota for this lifetime.''

It wasn't an answer. It wasn't even a good fake answer. She had the sudden thought that maybe he didn't know why he was doing it, either. Which was scary, but not as scary as having nowhere to go. It all came down to whether or not she trusted him. Ashley looked into his face, the strong bone structure, the empty eyes. He had a scar by his mouth and the few gray hairs at his temples. Both her gut and her daughter said he was safe. Was that enough?

''I'm a member of the Better Business Bureau. Does that help?''

The corners of his mouth turned up. The smile transformed him, making him handsome and approachable. It also made her heart beat just a little faster and her breathing increase.

The flu, she told herself. A physical manifestation of her virus. Nothing more.

''Thank you,'' she said, pushing herself to her feet and swaying slightly before she gained her balance. ''I'm very grateful for your assistance.''

''You're welcome.''

There was a plus to all this, she thought. If Jeff turned out to be a nice guy in disguise, maybe she could convince him not to fire her from her cleaning job. Then in a few short days, she could return to her regular life and pretend none of this had happened.

The security-soldier business paid better than she'd realized, Ashley thought thirty minutes later when Jeff pulled into the driveway of a two-story glass-and-wood house more than halfway up Queen Anne Hill. The view through clouds and light rain was impressive, with Lake Union down below and the west side of the city visible across the water. She could only imagine how beautiful it would be when the weather was nice.

"Is this yours?" Maggie asked excitedly from the back seat of the luxury car. "It's so big and pretty. Do you have kittens? There's lots of room for them. If you wanted to get one, I'd help you take very good care of it."

"Ever hopeful," Ashley murmured. "Maggie is desperate for a kitten."

"I've noticed."

On their way over from the shelter Maggie had talked about kittens and her school and how nice everyone at the shelter had been. It gave the adults a break from having to make conversation. Ashley, for one, was grateful.

"Where's your 'partment?" Maggie asked as they waited for the garage door to open. "Is it up high? Mommy and me live on the top floor and sometimes it's fun to look out at the city or watch when the storms come. And in the summer when it's hot, we open all the windows, 'cause no one can climb in when we're up so high."

Jeff turned off the engine and shifted to face the little girl. "It's a house, Maggie," he told her. "I live here by myself. While you and your mom stay here, I want you to be very comfortable."

Maggie's eyes widened. "It's just you here? Don'tcha get scared being all alone?"

Ashley winced. Until this moment she'd never realized that her daughter hadn't ever lived in a house before. They'd always been in apartments.

"Sometimes it's quiet," Jeff admitted. "But I don't mind that."

He was about to have a couple of days of nonquiet, Ashley thought. Maggie was a sweetheart and very well behaved, but she was a walking noise machine.

He unfastened his seat belt. "Let's get you two inside and settled. I'll bring your bags in later."

Ashley nodded. She could feel the weariness settling over her again. Her consciousness through the drive here had taken the last of her reserves. All she wanted was to sleep for the next four or five weeks.

Jeff climbed out of the car, then opened the rear door to assist Maggie from the vehicle. Ashley trailed after them as they went up the two stairs that led to the main house. Before he opened the door, Jeff punched a long code into a keypad. There was an audible *snick* as the locking mechanism released. She had a brief thought of armed guards waiting on the other side and chuckled at the image of them walking through metal detectors before entering the living quarters of the house.

But whatever security measures existed were concealed because all she saw when she stepped inside was space.

The rooms were huge and sparsely furnished. Jeff showed them the living room, dining room and a study. Only the latter contained any evidence that a person actually lived in the house. The living room had two sofas, a couple of club chairs, along with low tables and a few lamps. But there was nothing personal or decorative. No pictures or photographs on the walls, no magazines, plants or even a pair of shoes marred the solitude. The dining room was the same. A massive table surrounded by chairs. A matching hutch—the glassed-in top of which was empty.

Cream carpet and pale walls added to the sense of space, as did the floor-to-ceiling windows in both the living room and dining room that offered a view of the lake and the shore beyond. The study was at the rear of the house, looking out on extensive gardens. At least here there were papers on the desk and a few books scattered on the leather sofa across from the fireplace.

Ashley looked around without saying anything, then followed Jeff into his huge kitchen. She took in the oversized refrigerator, the six-burner stove and the impressive collection of copper pots hanging above the tiled island.

"You must entertain a lot," she murmured, not able to imagine such a thing. With someone else maybe, but not Jeff Ritter. He didn't appear to be the entertaining type.

"No. It all came with the house." He motioned to the refrigerator. "I eat out, or at the office. There isn't much in the way of food. When I get you settled, I'll take Maggie and go to the grocery store."

She wanted to protest. Surely there was enough for

them to get by until she was feeling better. She didn't want to impose. Impulsively she opened the refrigerator, about to make that point. However, the point went unmade.

The interior of the gleaming metal refrigerator was empty. Not just echoing with the stereotypical bachelor fare of beer and condiments. It was as empty as a showroom model. Ashley swallowed, then moved to the pantry. Those shelves were neatly papered and just as bare.

Jeff cleared his throat. "Like I said, I don't eat here much."

"Ever," she corrected. "How can you not have coffee?"

Instead of answering, he indicated that they should follow him toward the staircase at the rear of the house. On the landing it split in two directions. He took the stairs on the right.

"This is the guest wing," he said. "The two bedrooms share a bathroom."

He opened doors, leading the way to well-furnished bedrooms, one larger than the other. The bathroom setup gave them each a vanity and mirror, while they shared the toilet and bath. Maggie hurried to the window seat in the smaller room and knelt on the yellow cushion.

"I like this," she said, holding her stuffed cat close to her chest and smiling. "I can see the water."

"Good."

Ashley hoped her voice sounded pleased. She was having trouble forming the words as her strength faded. She made her way back into the larger of the two rooms. As it had been downstairs, the furniture was exactly right but there were no homey touches. The walls were blank, as were the surfaces of the dresser and nightstands, except for a clock radio silently illuminating the time.

Ashley found she didn't care about decorating or empty refrigerators. Exhaustion descended with no warning, sucking up the last of her strength, leaving her shaking and breathless.

Jeff seemed to figure out her problem. Without saying anything, he drew back the covers on the bed and urged her to sit on the clean sheet.

"You need sleep," he said, reaching for her shoes and tugging them off. "I'll take care of Maggie. Just rest."

She started to protest. She had to give her daughter instructions to be good, to listen to Jeff and to come running to her if she was afraid. Even as she stretched out on the bed she thought it might be a good idea to stay awake for a while to make sure everything was all right here in the beautiful house on the hill. She ought to—

Jeff watched Ashley fight against exhaustion. Slowly her eyes closed and her breathing slowed.

"We'll be going out for food," he murmured as she drifted off to sleep. "We'll be back soon."

She didn't respond. Maggie bounced into the room, her mouth open to speak. She stopped when she saw her mother asleep, pressing her lips together and then looking at him.

He walked to the door and motioned for her to follow. When they were out in the hall, he stared down at her, wondering what he was supposed to do now. Food, he thought. They had to get food. He hesitated, not sure if he'd ever gone grocery shopping before. As he'd told Ashley, he ate all his meals at restaurants, or at work. It's not that he didn't know how to keep food in the house, he simply didn't bother. Despite the furniture in the rooms and his clothes in his bedroom closet, this wasn't his home. It was a place to sleep and work after hours. Nothing more.

"We're going shopping," he announced. "The grocery store."

Maggie hesitated before nodding her agreement. She looked so small standing there in her pink jeans and pink-and-white plaid knit sweater. Two tiny clips held her dark curls off her face. Her Cupid's bow mouth quivered slightly.

Not knowing what else to do, Jeff crouched in front of the child. "You know your mom is sick, right?"

"Uh-huh." Her grip on the battered stuffed cat tightened.

"She has the flu. Do you know what that is?"

"It's what I had last week. I was very sick and I got to watch TV in Mommy's bed and eat Jell-O whenever I wanted."

Was that kid paradise? He didn't know. "But you're better now, right?"

Another nod.

"So you know your mom is going to be fine in a few days. I don't want you to worry about her."

Maggie gave him an impish smile. "I know you'll take care of her."

He hadn't thought about his responsibility in quite those terms, but if it made the kid happy to think that, he wouldn't disagree. "Are you nervous about being with me?"

Delicate, dark eyebrows drew together. "What's nerv-nerv-What's that?"

"Nervous. Upset. Afraid. Anxious." His explanation didn't seem to be helping. He searched his memory for a word a four-year-old could understand. "Scared."

This time, instead of smiling, she laughed. "I'm not scared. You *like* us."

She spoke with a conviction he both envied and admired. If only all of life were that simple, he thought as he rose to his full height.

"Then let's go to the food store."

Maggie trailed after him as they made their way to the car. Jeff hesitated, then decided not to set the alarm in the house. He figured the odds of Ashley opening a door or window were greater than someone breaking in during the short time he would be gone.

He held the back door open for the little girl, then helped her fasten her seat belt. She gazed at him trustingly as he secured her in the car. She sniffed loudly.

"Your car smells nice."

"It's the leather. I've only had the car a few months."

Her eyes widened. "It's new? You have a new car?"

Her tone of reverence made him wonder if Ashley had ever had a new car. Based on her current circumstances, he doubted it. At least not in the recent past. There were so many things in his life that he took for granted.

"I have to call someone I know," he said as he

slid into the driver's seat. "I need to ask her what to buy to make your mom feel better."

"Jell-O," Maggie said firmly.

"Okay, but she'll need other stuff, too." He was thinking in terms of liquids. Or was that for a cold? His first-aid training ran more in the direction of gunshot wounds or emergency amputations.

He backed out of the driveway, then touched a button. A mechanical voice asked, "What name?"

"Brenda," he replied.

Maggie stared at him. "The car is talking!"

He felt himself smile as the sound of a phone ringing came over the built-in speakers. It was nearly five-thirty. Brenda might have gone home.

But his assistant was still at the office. When she answered, he explained that he was taking care of a friend with the flu and needed her advice on what to buy at the grocery store. Also, what would be appropriate to serve a four-year-old for dinner.

With that he glanced at the girl. "Say hi, Maggie."

Still wide-eyed and clutching her stuffed, white cat, Maggie licked her lips. "Hi," she whispered tentatively.

"That was Maggie," he said helpfully.

"Uh, hi, Maggie. Nice to talk to you." His assistant's tone of voice warned him that he would be getting a major third degree when he saw her in the morning.

"Do you even know where the grocery store is?" Brenda asked when she'd recovered from her shock.

"I have a fair idea. I was thinking of soup and juice. Liquids for the flu, right?"

"Uh, yeah, that's right. As for dinner for the little

one, there are lots of options. Rule number one is the less sugar the better. Are you cooking or heating?''

Ten minutes later he had a list along with instructions. Brenda cleared her throat. ''Are they going to be staying with you for a few days?''

''Yes. Why?''

''If the mother isn't feeling well, then she won't be up to watching her child. Maggie, do you have a preschool you go to?''

The little girl beamed at being included in the conversation. ''Uh-huh. Right by Mommy's school. I stay there until two.''

''Ashley is a student at the University of Washington,'' he clarified.

''Which means she'll be missing class while she's sick.''

He heard Brenda writing on a pad of paper. ''Can we send someone to sit in for her?'' he asked.

''Sure, but I need her schedule of classes first. Some lecture notes are available online. Also, Maggie will need a sitter for the afternoon. I can arrange that. What's your student friend's name?''

''Ashley Churchill. She works for us.''

There was a moment of silence. Jeff could practically see Brenda's surprise. She knew everyone who worked for Ritter/Rankin Security.

''The cleaner?''

''Yes.''

''How did you meet her?'' She coughed. ''Sorry. It's not any of my business, of course. I'll get on all of this and call you later tonight.''

''Thanks, Brenda. I appreciate the effort.''

His assistant laughed. ''No problem. You know I'm

desperate to break into the spy business. There has to be a market for fifty-something operatives. Finding this information will be good practice.''

"I'd be lost without you in the office. I can't afford to let you go into the field.''

"So you keep saying. But I think you're just being kind and trying to not hurt my feelings. Oh, well. I'll call you later, Jeff. Bye, Maggie.''

"Bye,'' Maggie piped back.

Jeff disconnected the call, then wondered how Brenda could ever be foolish enough to think of him as kind.

Chapter Three

"They're very good," Maggie said earnestly.

They stood in the cereal aisle of the large grocery store just down the hill from Jeff's house. He'd never been inside in all the time he'd lived in the neighborhood. He doubted Maggie had been here, either, yet she led the way like an expert, wielding her miniature shopping cart around other patrons, calling out names of favorite brands and making decisions with the ease of an executive. Now she held out a box of Pop-Tarts and gave him a winning smile.

"I had them at Sara's house. Her mom fixed them for us. She said only kids could eat something that purple." Her smile broadened. "I said that the purple is the best part."

He looked doubtfully at the picture on the box. It showed a toaster pastry covered with vivid purple frosting. Just the thought made his stomach tighten. In this case, he'd have to side with Sara's mom.

"You really want those?" he asked, not sure how that was possible.

Maggie nodded vigorously, making her dark curls dance around her head.

"Does your mother buy these for you?"

Big blue eyes suddenly turned away from him. She became intensely interested in the contents of her cart, rearranging the three frozen kid meals he'd bought her. Finally she returned her gaze to him and slowly shook her head.

"No."

Outside of his abilities, he didn't count on very much in the world, but he would have bet his life that Maggie Churchill was incapable of lying—whether because of her age, her character, her upbringing or a combination of the three. He didn't think he'd ever met anyone like her before.

"Would you really eat them if we got them?"

Questions filled her eyes. Questions and hope. She practically vibrated her assent.

"All right." He tossed the package into her tiny cart. "If you're sure."

She gazed at him as if he'd just created a rainbow right there in the grocery store. She threw herself at him, wrapping her arms around his legs and squeezing tight.

"Thank you," she said fervently. "I'll be good. I promise."

He hadn't known she could be anything but.

They continued their shopping, going up and down each aisle. Jeff found that buying bread for sandwiches also meant buying something to go in between the slices of bread. Maggie favored peanut butter and jelly. He thought her mother might appreciate something more along the lines of sliced turkey or beef. Which meant an intense discussion on mustard versus mayonnaise, and an interpretation of whether or not Maggie's shudder at the thought of pickles meant her mother didn't like them, either.

The girl's cart was already full and his was nearly so when they turned the corner and found themselves in the pet food aisle. Maggie touched a can of cat food and sighed.

"Do you have a kitty?" she asked, sounding hopeful. "I didn't see one but maybe she was asleep."

"Sorry. No pets."

"Why? Don'tcha like them?"

"Cats?" He'd never thought about them one way or the other. Dogs could be a problem. Dogs made noise, alerting people to the presence of intruders. More than one mission had nearly been compromised by the unexpected presence of a dog. But cats?

"I travel a lot," he said, then hesitated. Conversing with Maggie was both easy and difficult. He didn't mind spending time in her company, which surprised him, but he wasn't sure what to say. How did people talk to children? He only knew how to talk to adults.

"Pets are a big responsibility," he continued. "It wouldn't be fair to the animal to leave it alone all the time."

She considered his statement, then nodded slowly. "Mommy and I are home plenty, but she says we can't have a kitten just yet. They can be expensive. Not for her food, but if she got sick or somethin'.

Mommy gets sad about money sometimes. She cries in the bathroom.'' Maggie pressed her lips together. ''I don't think I'm supposed to know, but I can hear her, even with the water running. Can you make Mommy not be sad?''

He wasn't sure what to do with the information Maggie shared. Based on the little he knew about Ashley's situation, he wasn't surprised by her financial concerns. But he also wasn't willing to take on responsibility for her emotional state.

''Your mother isn't sad now,'' he said, sidestepping the issue.

Maggie thought for a moment, then nodded her agreement. ''Mommy's happy.''

Jeff thought that might be a stretch. Ashley might be relieved to be out of the shelter, but he doubted she was pleased with her present circumstances. His guess was she wouldn't rest easy until she had her life back in order.

While Jeff heated soup in a pan on the stove, Maggie watched her frozen kid's dinner as it warmed in the microwave. The entrée had come with a small toy, which she clutched in her hand as she danced from foot to foot, waiting for the timer to beep.

''I like chicken,'' she announced. ''And macaroni and cheese. I've never had them together before.''

It didn't sound like much of a treat to him, but then, he wasn't four. After stirring Ashley's soup, he returned to the task of putting away the rest of the groceries. As the pantry shelves were bare, it didn't take long. He put milk and juice into the refrigerator, along with several cartons of yogurt. Frozen foods went into the freezer.

Grocery shopping and cooking had to be two of the most normal activities, and yet they all felt foreign to him. He didn't eat yogurt from a carton. The last time he'd had the stuff had been during a covert operation in Afghanistan and the goat responsible for the yogurt had watched him warily, as if to make sure he swallowed every spoonful.

He stirred the soup again, then checked on Maggie's dinner.

"Twenty more seconds," she told him, never taking her gaze from the timer.

He dug through kitchen cupboards, pulling out a bowl from a set of dishes he doubted he'd ever used. He also unearthed a wooden tray. After rinsing and drying the bowl, he poured the soup, then, along with a spoon, set it on the tray, next to some toast and a glass of juice. When the microwave beeped, he lifted Maggie's dinner onto the tray, along with cutlery and a drink, and started toward his guest's room.

"I get dessert later, right?" Maggie asked, confirming the reality of her purple Pop-Tart.

"Absolutely. We'll get your mom settled first, though."

"Okay."

He waited while Maggie pushed open the door, then he stepped into Ashley's room. Light spilled out from the bathroom, but the bedroom itself was in twilight. He could make out her still figure on the bed. Her eyes were closed, her breathing even.

He was about to retreat, taking Maggie with him,

when the four-year-old flew at her mother and pounced onto the mattress.

"Mommy, Mommy, we brought dinner. There's soup for you and chicken pieces and macaroni and cheese for me. And Mr. Ritter got me Pop-Tarts and they're *purple!*"

Ashley came awake slowly. She opened her eyes and smiled at her daughter, then shifted her gaze so she could take in the room. He both felt and saw the exact moment she noticed him. For a second she looked confused, then she blinked and the questions in her eyes were gone.

Jeff was pleased she didn't appear frightened. He doubted the circumstances were to her liking, but she was in no condition to change them. He'd said and done as much as he could to convince her she was completely safe in his company, but it would take time and experience for her to learn that she could trust him.

"I brought dinner," he said as he flipped on the floor lamp. "Do you think you can eat?"

"I'm going to eat with you," Maggie said, sliding off the bed and walking to the small table by the window. "Is here okay?"

"It's fine, sweetie." Ashley shifted until she was in a sitting position, her back against the headboard. She rubbed her eyes, then looked at the tray. "I'm not hungry, but I haven't had anything since dinner last night, so I should probably try to get something down."

He served Maggie first, carefully putting her entrée in front of her, then setting out a fork, a glass of milk and three napkins. When he carried the tray to Ashley, he noticed that she'd changed her clothes while they'd been gone. She'd traded jeans for sweatpants and her blouse for a loose T-shirt, both in faded navy.

She was pale, with dark circles under her eyes. Sleep had mussed her dark hair. While it wasn't as curly as her daughter's, it was thick and wavy, falling just to her shoulders.

"Maggie promised that you like chicken soup," he said adjusting the tray so the legs bracketed Ashley's slender thighs.

"What's not to like?" she said, picking up a spoon and taking a sip. "It's great." She paused and looked at him. "You've been more than kind. I really appreciate it. We'll be out of your hair by morning."

"I doubt that," Jeff told her. "You're sick. You're going to need a few days to get your strength back. I want you to feel comfortable enough to do that here."

Her hazel eyes seemed more blue than green or brown. Was it the hour of the day or a reflection of her navy T-shirt? Her arms were thin…too thin. Maggie had a sturdiness about her, but Ashley looked as if a slight breeze could blow her away.

As he continued to stare, he noticed a flush of color climbing her cheeks. At first he thought it was from her fever, but then he had the sudden thought that she might be uncomfortable with his scrutiny. He shifted his attention to her daughter.

"Maggie was a big help at the grocery store," he said. The little girl beamed at him.

"I can only imagine," Ashley said dryly. "She convinced you to buy Pop-Tarts."

"I wasn't a hard sell."

"Mr. Ritter has a magic car," Maggie said between bites of chicken. "A lady spoke to us from the air and everything."

Jeff pulled out the second chair at the small table and sat down. "I called my assistant from the car, using the speakerphone. I needed some menu ideas."

"She was very nice and said hello to me," Maggie added.

The girl had finished most of her macaroni and cheese, although she wore a good portion of the sauce on her face and hands. Jeff studied the shape of her eyes and her mouth, then glanced at her mother, trying to figure out what traits they shared.

Ashley's features were slightly more delicate. The eye color was different, as well. Did Maggie's blue eyes come from her father?

Ashley tucked a strand of hair behind her ear, using her left hand. Jeff had already noted that she didn't wear a ring, but now he looked to see if there were any telltale marks showing one had recently been removed. He didn't see any tan lines or indentations. A divorce? he wondered. Although having a baby didn't require a woman to marry, Ashley struck him as the marrying kind. He didn't think she would have chosen to have a child on her own. Not without a good reason.

"Is there anyone I should phone?" he asked. "A relative out of state, a friend?"

She paused in the act of drinking her juice and carefully put down the glass. "You mean to let them know where I am?"

"Yes."

A shadow slipped across her eyes and she looked

away from him. He could read her mind as clearly as if she spoke her thoughts. The truthful answer was that she was all alone in the world. If there was no one to care about her, then there was no one to worry if she and her daughter disappeared.

He leaned toward her. "I'm not going to hurt you, Ashley."

She smiled without meeting his gaze. He hated that the fear was back in her eyes. "I know. I wasn't thinking that at all. You've been very good to us."

"Your parents?" he asked, knowing he shouldn't pry.

"Grandma's in heaven with Daddy," Maggie piped up. She'd finished her dinner and was carefully wiping her hands with a napkin.

Ashley a widow? Jeff frowned. She was too young, barely in her mid-twenties. What had happened? A car accident? Murder? Did her husband's death account for her difficult financial circumstances?

Before he could decide if he could ask any or all of those questions, his cell phone rang. He excused himself and stepped into the hall.

"Ritter," he said into the instrument.

"It's Brenda," his assistant said. "I have been my normal efficient self. Are you ready?"

"Just a second." He pulled a notebook and a pen from his suit pocket and started walking toward his study downstairs. "Go ahead."

"I've found a sitter for Maggie tomorrow afternoon. It's one of her teachers from the preschool. So not only is the woman qualified and trustworthy, but Maggie already knows and likes her. Next, I have Ashley's schedule of classes in front of me. She has two tomorrow. They're advanced classes and don't have Internet lecture notes so I've been in touch with an off-campus service that specializes in taking notes. They will attend both lectures for her and provide me with typed notes by two tomorrow afternoon.''

"I'm impressed," he said, sliding behind his desk and settling on his leather chair. "How'd you find her class schedule?"

Brenda chuckled. "I was about to get all high-tech and then I remembered she works here. Her Social Security number is on the job application in her personnel file. After that, it was easy. After all, I've learned from the best.''

"Do you mean me or Zane?"

"I refuse to answer that," she said, her voice teasing. "I'll drop by about seven tomorrow morning to help get the little one ready.''

"Do you think that's necessary? She seems fairly self-sufficient.'' After all, she'd talked him into getting just about everything she wanted at the grocery store.

"Do you really want to deal with getting a four-year-old girl ready for school? I'm talking about picking out clothes and doing her hair.''

He hadn't thought that part through. "I guess not. Seven sounds fine. I appreciate this, Brenda.''

"I know. I just wish you'd let me go into the field. I'd be great.''

"Your husband would kill me.''

"Probably, but I'd have a fabulous time.''

He tried to imagine his fifty-something assistant slinking along the banks of a Russian river, waiting to make a drop.

Brenda sighed. "I know, I know. I don't speak any languages, I'm wildly out of shape, but hey, a girl can dream, right?"

"Absolutely. And comfort yourself with the thought that I'd be lost without you."

"I know." She chuckled. "See you in the morning, boss."

"We'll be here."

He pushed the "end" button and terminated the call, then went back upstairs so he could return to Ashley's room and collect the tray.

He found the larger guest room empty and the sound of running water and laughter coming from the bathroom. Jeff quickly picked up empty dishes and set them on the tray. He was nearly out the door when Ashley appeared.

"I thought I heard you return," she said, leaning against the wall by the bathroom. "Thanks for making dinner. I'm going to give Maggie a bath, then come down with her while she has her dessert. We'll read for a bit and both be in bed by eight."

Weariness darkened her eyes and pulled at the corners of her mouth. She was attractive, in a slender, delicate sort of way.

"You look like you could use a good night's sleep," he said.

She studied him. "I can't decide if I should ask you again why you're bothering, or simply be grateful."

"How about just thinking about getting well?"

She tilted her head slightly. "My daughter thinks you're a very nice man."

"Your daughter is trusting." Too trusting.

''She hasn't had a chance to learn otherwise.''

She'd made a statement but he wondered if it was also a warning. As in *Don't teach her differently. Don't give her a reason not to trust.*

Jeff wanted to reassure her that he had no intention of destroying Maggie's illusions about the world. Time would take care of that, and far too quickly for his taste. Oddly, he liked knowing that somewhere a four-year-old little girl laughed with glee because there were Pop-Tarts and kittens.

''Who are you, Jeff Ritter?''

No one you want to know. But he didn't say that aloud because it would frighten her. ''A friend.''

''I hope so. Good night.''

She turned back to the bathroom. He left her bedroom and walked down to the kitchen where he loaded the dirty dishes into the dishwasher then thought about fixing dinner for himself. There were sandwich ingredients and frozen dinners, soup, chili and a couple of apples.

But instead of preparing a meal, he walked into the living room and stared out into the night. The light rain had stopped although clouds still covered the sky. Jeff looked into the darkness, trying to ignore the sense of impending doom. He felt the familiar clenching of his gut and knew that trouble lay ahead. As he wasn't on a mission, he didn't know what form the trouble would take. Obviously it had something to do with the woman. With Ashley.

Even from this distance, he could sense her in the house. Her soft scent drifted through the air, teasing him, making him wonder how it would feel to be like other men.

* * *

His footsteps crunched on the path that led through the center of the village. It was night, yet he could see everything clearly. Probably because of the fire.

The flames were everywhere, licking at the edges of the shabby structures, chasing after the unwary residents, occasionally catching someone off guard and consuming them in a heartbeat.

The fire was alive, fueled by dry timbers and a chemical dreamed up in a lab thousands of miles away. Jeff was familiar with the smell, the heat and the destruction. He hated the fire. It showed no mercy. At times he would swear he heard it laughing as it destroyed.

It was only after he'd gone into the center square of the village that he became aware of the sounds. The *crack* of timbers breaking as they were consumed, the gunshot sound of glass exploding, the screams of the villagers. The soft crying of a lost child.

He knew this village. Every building, every person. He knew that just beyond the rise in the path was the river. He could walk through the fire again and again and never be touched. Because this village was a part of him, a creation of his mind and he was drawn to it night after night. No matter how he fought against the dream, it pulled him in, sucking him toward hell as surely as the fire crept toward the truck at the edge of the square and caught it in its grasp.

A sharp cry caught his attention. He turned and saw a teenage girl running from a burning building. A support beam creaked and tipped, then fell toward her. Jeff saw it happen in slow motion. He took one step, then another. He reached for the girl, determined to pull her to safety. He put out his hand.

She reached toward him in response. Slowly, achingly slowly, she raised her head until she could see him. Then her mouth opened wider and she screamed as he'd never heard another human being scream before. Sheer, soul-numbing terror.

She jerked away from him and ran toward the river. The support beam tumbled to the ground, narrowly missing her as she fled. Jeff took a step after her. Only then did he notice that all the villagers were racing away from him. They pointed and screamed, acting as if he were a threat worse than the fire.

An aching coldness filled him. Unable to stop himself, he walked toward the river, toward the small pool fed by the flowing water. Fire raged all around him, but he remained untouched by the destruction. People ran past him, screaming, darting out of his way. A mother raced by, a toddler in her arms. The small child cried when he saw Jeff, then ducked his head into the curve of his mother's neck.

They ran and ran until he was alone. Alone and standing by the pool. And even though he didn't want to look, he couldn't help himself. He knelt by the still water and waited for the smoke to clear enough for him to see his reflection.

Then he knew why they ran, why they screamed in terror. He wasn't a man. Instead of his face, he saw the cold metal features of a mechanical creature. A robot. A metal being not even remotely alive. Fire danced over him, but he couldn't feel it. Nor did it hurt him. He couldn't be burned or damaged in any way. He could only terrify…

Jeff woke in a cold sweat, the way he did every night after the dream. There was no moment of confusion. From the second consciousness returned, he knew exactly where he was and what had happened. He also knew he wouldn't sleep for several hours.

He rose and, in deference to his company, pulled on jeans and a sweatshirt. Then he left his bedroom, prepared to wander through the house like a ghost. Silent, alone, living in the shadows. He tried not to think about the dream, but he was, as usual, unsuccessful. He knew what it meant—that he didn't see himself as human. That he considered himself little more than a machine of destruction. But knowing the truth of the message wasn't enough to make it stop.

As he moved down the hall, he felt a change in the night air. Not a disturbance, just something…different. He could sense the presence of his guests.

Unable to stop himself, he headed in the direction of their rooms. Maggie's door was partially closed. He stood in the hallway and looked in on her.

She slept in the center of the double bed, a small figure guarded by her menagerie of stuffed animals. She was curled up, the blankets tucked around her, sleeping soundly, breathing evenly. A dark curl brushed against her cheek.

He remembered her trust, the sound of her laughter, her delight at the speakerphone in his car. She was a magical child, he thought gruffly, as he noticed one of her fluffy cats had tumbled to the ground. Silently he stepped into her room and put the toy back on the bed. Then, because he couldn't stop himself, he moved through the connecting bathroom and into Ashley's room.

Her sleep was more troubled than her daughter's. She moved under the covers. Her face was slightly flushed, but when he touched her forehead, he didn't feel any heat.

Who was this woman with no family and such dire circumstances? From what he could observe, she was bright and capable. What had happened to bring her to the place where she needed to depend upon his good graces?

Knowing he wasn't going to get any answers, he left her room and walked downstairs. In the living room he walked to the windows and stared out into the night. For the first time since he'd moved into the house, he wasn't alone. How strange. He was always alone. No one came here. Certainly no one had spent the night. When there were women, he visited *them.* He had an animal's need to protect its territory. Yet he had been the one to invite Ashley and her daughter here in the first place. What did that mean?

He asked the question and received no answer. So he moved into his study where he turned on his computer. Ashley Churchill intrigued him. So he would find out what he needed with his special programs and secret information. When all was revealed to him she would cease to be anything but a woman and then he could easily let her go.

Chapter Four

The normally silent morning was filled with changes. Jeff stood in his kitchen, sipping a cup of coffee made in a coffeemaker he hadn't known he owned until he went looking for it a half hour before. Generally he simply got up, showered, dressed and left for the office. He was usually the first one in the building and made coffee when he arrived. He felt strange still being at home when it was almost seven-thirty.

From upstairs came the sound of movement and laughter. Brenda had shown up promptly at seven and was getting Maggie ready for preschool. Jeff glanced at his watch and realized he should check on Ashley before they left. He needed to make sure she would be all right on her own during the day.

He set his coffee mug on the counter then headed

for the stairs. Sleep had taken longer than usual to reclaim him the previous night. He'd been unable to forget he had guests in his house. He couldn't decide if their presence was good, bad or simply different.

He paused outside of Ashley's door and knocked once. A muffled voice invited him to enter. He stepped inside and found Ashley sitting on the edge of her bed. She looked sleepy and flushed. Her hair was mussed and weariness tugged at her mouth, but she held clothes in her arms as if she planned on getting dressed and starting her day.

"How do you feel?" he asked.

"Great. Much better. Thanks."

She was such a lousy liar, he nearly smiled. "Sell it somewhere else. You look dead on your feet and you're not even standing."

She brushed her hair off her face. "I have to get up. Maggie has school and so do I. She needs to get dressed and have breakfast. I have my own classes to attend. Plus, you've already been so kind. I don't want to impose any longer."

Determination stiffened her small frame. She raised her chin slightly, in a gesture of defiance that reminded him of a kitten spitting at a wolf. It looked great and accomplished nothing, except possibly amusing the wolf.

Instead of answering Ashley directly, he called for Brenda to join him.

Brenda bustled into the room. His assistant, a fifty-something blonde of medium height, was dressed in tailored slacks and a silk blouse. She looked efficient and ran his office with the precision and attention to detail of a neurosurgeon at work.

She walked to Ashley and held out her hand. "Hi. I'm Brenda Maitlin. You must be Ashley. Your daughter is such a sweetheart. And you look like death, honey."

Ashley had responded to Brenda's greeting by shaking hands with the woman. As Jeff watched, his assistant took the pile of clothes from Ashley and set them on the dresser. She maneuvered the other woman back under the covers and pulled up the blankets.

"Don't think about anything," Brenda instructed her. "Just sleep and get better."

"But I have to get my daughter dressed and take her to school. Then—"

Brenda cut her off with a quick shake of her head. "You don't have to do a darned thing. Maggie has been fed and dressed. I'm dropping her off at her preschool on my way to the office. Maggie's sitter, one of her teachers from school, is going to look after her after school at her place." She paused as if going through a mental list before continuing. "Oh, and a note taker will go to class for you today, so you don't have to worry about that, either." She turned to Jeff and beamed. "I think that's everything."

Ashley looked stunned. Jeff winked at her. "I know Brenda can be a little overwhelming, but that's why I hired her. Get the best people possible to do the job."

Brenda looked at him. "Then I have just two words to say to you. Field work."

It was an old argument. "I have just one word in response. No. I'd miss you in the office and your husband would kill me."

She glared at him before stomping out of the room.

Jeff returned his attention to Ashley. "She's convinced she would make a great spy. I suspect she's right, but she's late in starting her training and I doubt her family would approve."

Ashley looked confused, as if she was having a difficult time following the conversation. Before she could respond, Maggie burst into the room. The little girl was dressed in purple jeans with a matching purple-and-white sweater. Tiny clips held her hair off of her face. She grinned at Jeff before racing to her mother.

"Mommy, Mommy, Brenda came and cooked me breakfast. We had waffles and I ate a whole one. Then we got me dressed and now I'm going to school in her car. She's got a dog named Muffin and maybe when you feel better we can go visit them."

"A whole waffle. I'm impressed." Ashley raised up on one elbow to study her daughter. "Are you all right?" she asked. "Did you sleep well?"

Maggie laughed. "Mommy, I'm fine." She gave her a quick hug, then dashed out of the room.

Ashley lowered herself back onto the bed. "Thanks for taking care of her. And of me. You're being very nice."

"No one has ever accused me of that before."

"Probably because you didn't give them reason."

Her eyes fluttered closed. Her skin looked soft and smooth. He had an instant vision of touching her cheek, then her mouth. The image was so real, his fingertips burned. Suddenly uncomfortable, he took a step back and tried to figure out what to say.

"I'll be at the office all day," he told her. "Will you be all right by yourself?"

"Sure. I just need to rest a little more."

"The kitchen is well stocked. Take whatever you'd like." He set a business card on the nightstand. "Here's my number, in case you need it."

She nodded slowly, her eyes drifting closed. He knew the exact moment she found sleep. For a second he thought about giving in and touching her cheek…just to see if it was as soft as it looked. But he didn't. Men like him didn't have physical contact with women like her. Men like him remembered they weren't the same as everyone else. And if he tried to forget, the dream was a constant reminder.

Ashley rolled over and glanced at the digital clock on the nightstand: 7:01…a.m. She blinked. As in the morning? She sat up with a hastiness that made her head spin. Morning? That wasn't possible. She last remembered it being seven-thirty in the morning. Had she really slept around the clock?

She threw back the covers and slid to her feet. Aside from a little light-headedness that was probably due to not eating in thirty-six hours, she felt a whole lot better than she had before. But all thoughts of health were pushed aside by the panicky realization she hadn't seen her daughter since the previous morning.

She flew through the shared bathroom and into the adjoining room. It was empty. Empty! Panic tightened her throat. Dear God, what had happened to her daughter? Her eyes began to burn as tears formed. "Maggie," she whispered. "Maggie?"

Just was she was about to scream, she heard a faint sound. She spun in that direction and realized it came from downstairs. There was a low rumble of a male voice followed by childish laughter.

Maggie!

Relief flooded her. Ashley hurried into the hall and made her way to the stairs. Ignoring the shaking in her legs and the dizziness that lingered, she ran down the stairs and raced into the kitchen. With one sweeping glance, she saw her daughter sitting at the table and eating a triangle of toast and jam.

"Maggie!"

Her little girl looked up and smiled with delight. "Mommy, you're up! I wanted to see you last night but Uncle Jeff said you needed to sleep so I was very quiet when I came to say good-night."

As she spoke, Maggie slid off her chair and hurried to her mother. Ashley took in the mismatched shirt and jeans, the smudge of jam on the girl's cheek and the crooked clips in her hair. Her heart filled with love as she gathered her close and held her tightly.

"I love you, baby girl," she murmured, inhaling the familiar scent of her child.

"I love you, too, Mommy," her daughter whispered in response.

Still holding her child, Ashley looked past her to the man sitting at the table. His suit slacks were immaculate, as was his white shirt. His gray eyes seemed to see down to her receding panic. Which was crazy. He couldn't have known that she'd freaked when she'd awakened and Maggie hadn't been in her room. Could he?

"Brenda was delayed by a family crisis," he said.

"So we had to get ready without her." He nodded at Maggie. "She picked out her clothes and got herself dressed without any assistance. I did her hair." He smiled self-deprecatingly. "But you probably figured that out."

His smile did something funny to her insides. Or maybe it was just lack of food. Ashley released her daughter and studied her clothes and hair.

"It's perfect," she said.

Maggie beamed. "I've been extra good for Uncle Jeff. I ate all my cereal and I'm going to finish my toast and milk."

Ashley looked at their host. "Uncle Jeff?"

He shrugged. "Mr. Ritter seemed a little formal. I hope you don't mind."

"No. It's fine."

Weird, but fine. She had a hard time imagining Jeff Ritter as an uncle, but he'd obviously done well with Maggie.

He rose to his feet and pulled out a chair. "You must be starving. Let me get you some food."

Ashley was suddenly aware that she'd jumped out of bed without a thought for her appearance. She hadn't showered in two days or brushed her teeth, and her hair probably looked like a rat's nest.

"I, ah, think I'd like to take a shower first," she said, backing out of the room. She glanced at the clock on the wall. "Give me ten minutes."

Because of her recent illness, she wasn't moving as fast as usual, so it was closer to twenty before she walked back downstairs. Her first glance in the mirror hadn't been as horrible as it could have been, but she hadn't been in the position to win any beauty prizes, either. Now she was at least clean, with her hair washed, although still a little damp. Her face was too pale and way too thin. With the onset of the flu, Ashley hadn't been eating regularly for several days. Which meant a loss of weight she couldn't afford. Her jeans were already hanging on her.

She made her way into the kitchen and found Maggie dancing from foot to foot.

"Brenda called," she sang. "She called and she's on her way to take me to school. And—" she paused dramatically before making the most monumental of announcements "—she's bringing one of her dogs with her. The little one. Her name is Muffin and I get to hold her in the car!"

As Maggie spoke, she raced toward Ashley and threw herself at her. Automatically Ashley reached for her daughter, pulling her into her arms. But two days in bed and general weakness from the flu had sucked up all her strength. She staggered slightly and felt herself start to slip.

From the corner of her eye Ashley caught a blur of moment. Suddenly a strong arm encircled her waist, holding her upright. She found herself leaning against Jeff. She had a brief impression of heat and formidable muscles even as he led her to a chair by the table and eased her onto the seat. And then he was back in his chair with a speed that left her wondering if she'd imagined the whole thing.

Except that the left side of her burned from where she'd pressed against him, and she could almost feel his arm around her waist. She shivered slightly. Not from cold, but from... Ashley frowned. She wasn't sure what. Awareness? Because she was suddenly very aware of the man sitting across from her. He didn't seem as much the cold, mysterious stranger this morning.

Maggie shifted on her lap. "Do you think Muffin will like me?"

"How could she not?" Ashley asked. "You're an adorable little girl."

Her daughter beamed with delight. Before she could speak again, there was a loud rap at the front door, followed by the sound of steps on the entryway.

"It's me," a woman called. "Brace yourself, Jeff. I have a dog with me."

Her announcement was unnecessary. A bundle of fur careened around the corner and skittered into the kitchen. The creature was small—maybe seven or eight pounds of multicolored hair and big, brown eyes. At the sight of the animal, Maggie scrambled off Ashley's lap and dropped to her knees. The little dog beelined for the child and sniffed her outstretched fingers, then licked the tips and jumped against Maggie, yipping and licking and wiggling with delight.

"Muffin loves kids," Brenda said as she walked into the kitchen. "But then you probably guessed that." She looked at Ashley. "You seem better."

"I feel better, thanks." Ashley smiled, feeling slightly awkward. While she'd never met Brenda before yesterday, the woman was an employee of Ritter/Rankin Security. What must she think of Jeff bringing a fellow worker into his house and caring for her and her child while she was ill? She felt as if she had to explain the situation, but she didn't know what to say about it.

Brenda handed Jeff a folder. "I'd better get this

little one to her preschool,'' she said. ''See you at the office.''

He took the folder. ''Thanks, Brenda. I appreciate this.''

She grinned. ''Remember this the next time I request an assignment.''

''Yeah, right.''

Brenda rolled her eyes, then collected her dog. Maggie scrambled to her feet. ''Bye, Mommy. See you when I'm done with school.''

They hugged briefly, then Ashley waved as her daughter headed for the front door. ''Have a good day,'' she called after her.

As the front door closed, bread popped out of the toaster. Ashley started to get up but Jeff motioned her back into her seat.

''You're still recovering,'' he told her. ''Until yesterday morning I didn't even know I had a toaster. But that doesn't mean I don't know how to use it.''

He rose and put the two pieces of toast onto a plate. Butter and jam already sat on the table. He set the plate in front of her, then poured her a mug of coffee.

''Milk, sugar?''

''Black is fine,'' she said, slightly confused by his solicitousness.

He set the mug by her left hand, then resumed his seat. ''Eat,'' he said, pointing at the food.

Cautiously she reached for the butter and picked up a piece of toast. This was all too strange. What was she doing in this man's house? Although based on the fact that she'd already spent two nights here, it seemed a little late to be asking questions.

''I spoke with Maggie's teacher yesterday after

noon,'' Jeff said when she began to eat. ''I was told she didn't seem to be suffering any ill effects from being in a strange place.''

''Cathy spoke with you?'' The preschool had a strict policy of dealing only with parents or legal guardians.

Jeff raised his eyebrows. ''Why wouldn't she?''

A simple enough question. Jeff was the kind of man who got what he wanted. That much was obvious from the way he'd brought her and Maggie here, despite her protestations and concerns.

''I'm glad Maggie is doing well,'' she said in an effort to avoid his question.

''She is. Last night we had spaghetti and salad for dinner. She had a Pop-Tart for dessert.''

It might have been her imagination, but Jeff seemed to shudder. She felt herself smile slightly.

''I did not,'' he continued.

''No real surprise there,'' she murmured.

A slight upward tilt of the corner of his mouth was his only response. ''Then we watched *The Little Mermaid* on DVD. We'd stopped at Blockbuster on our way home from the sitter's. Maggie was in bed by eight and asleep by 8:10.''

Before she could comment, he passed her the folder Brenda had brought him. ''Here are your notes from your classes yesterday. If you're not well enough to attend classes tomorrow, I'll have Brenda arrange for someone to sit in for you. Also—'' he took a sip of coffee ''—I sent someone over to your apartment building to collect more of your belongings. You'll find them stacked in the living room.''

She flipped through the notes—typed and in perfect

order—then looked at him. She didn't know what to say. The man had completely organized her life, and made it look simple in the process. She thought of how her daughter had been dressed and fed in plenty of time that morning. He'd prepared dinner the previous night and provided entertainment. By comparison, all the men she'd ever known were incredibly incompetent.

"Maggie's father couldn't even find the clean diapers to change her," she said, "and he sure wouldn't be able to get her ready for school. How do you know how to do all this?"

"I had help from Brenda. She's raised four kids of her own and has a couple of grandchildren. Besides, compared to an antiterrorist campaign, running your life is easy."

"It's anything but that for me," she murmured, thinking it was not possible for their worlds to be more different. "Anything else?"

"Yes. Maggie's class is taking a field trip to the zoo next Friday. The permission slip had to be back yesterday for Maggie to go, so I signed it. Is that all right?"

Ashley sighed. "Of course. I'd meant to take care of that last week. I guess with her being sick and everything else that happened, I just forgot. She would have been heartbroken to miss the trip."

She studied her host. He wasn't just physically strong and a little scary, he was also incredibly competent. She needed that in her life right now, and the urge to let him take over and handle everything nearly overwhelmed her. No one had been around to look out for her since she was twelve.

A nice fantasy, she told herself, but one that had no basis in reality. The truth was she was an employee of Jeff Ritter. For reasons that still weren't clear to her, he'd taken her and her daughter and was making them feel very welcome in his beautiful home. But gracious or not, he was a stranger with a past that made her more than a little nervous.

"You've been really terrific," she said, then took a drink of coffee. "I'm feeling a lot better today. I'm sure that I'll be a hundred percent tomorrow and then we'll be out of your hair." She cleared her throat. "Would it be too much trouble to have someone bring my car here?"

Jeff studied her for a long time. As usual, not a flicker of thought or emotion showed in his steel-gray eyes. He could have been planning sixty-seven ways to kill her with household appliances or deciding on a second cup of coffee. She really hoped it was the latter.

She returned the scrutiny, noting the short, blond hair brushed back from his face and the high cheekbones. He was tall, muscled and extremely goodlooking. So why did he live alone in this gorgeous house? Was there a former Mrs. Ritter somewhere? Or was Jeff not the marrying kind? She bit her lower lip. As closemouthed and mysterious as he seemed, she could understand his avoiding a long-term commitment. Was there a series of significant girlfriends? And more importantly, why did she care?

Before she could come up with an answer to the question, he spoke.

"I'm glad you're feeling better, but getting over the flu is no reason to rush off."

His voice was low and well modulated. Controlled, she thought. Everything about him was controlled.

"I think it would be better if we left," she told him.

"Why? Do you really want Maggie living in a shelter until your apartment is fixed?"

Of course she didn't. It wasn't anyone's dream of a housing situation, but she didn't have a choice.

"Maggie is resilient. She'll be fine."

"Agreed, but I don't see the need to expose her to that. Why not stay here until your housing problem is resolved? There's plenty of room. You won't be in the way."

"But you don't know us. We're not family. I don't understand why you're—"

His pager went off before she could finish her sentence. Jeff glanced at the screen of the tiny machine, then rose to his feet.

"I have to leave," he told her. "Try to get plenty of rest so you can build up your strength."

Before she could say anything else, he'd grabbed his suit jacket from its place on the spare chair and left the room. Seconds later she heard a door close as he walked into the garage.

"How convenient," she muttered, nearly convinced he'd somehow arranged for his pager to go off at that exact moment. Which was crazy. Even someone like Jeff couldn't do that.

She finished her breakfast, then cleaned the kitchen. After wiping down the counters for the second time, she figured she might as well take a look at the rest of the house before she began studying

Not Jeff's bedroom or anything private, but just to get a lay of the land.

Jeff had made it clear they were welcome to stay until her apartment was fixed. Which could be a few more days. If she got more comfortable in his house, she might be more comfortable with the man. After all he'd been right about the shelter. It would be far better for Maggie to stay here than to move again.

She wandered through the main floor of the house. There was a large, formal living room with floor-to-ceiling glass windows overlooking the lake. The furniture was expensive, well made and completely impersonal. Her initial impression had been dead-on. There weren't any personal effects anywhere.

The dining room's cherry table could seat twelve, but Ashley had the feeling no one had ever eaten on it. In the family room she found state-of-the-art entertainment equipment, but no books or compact discs. The only movies were the ones he'd rented with Maggie.

Ashley paused in the center of the oversize room. The sectional sofa sat opposite the wide-screen television. There weren't any photographs or paintings. Nothing personal. Who was Jeffrey Ritter and why did he live like this? It was as if he had no past—but instead had appeared fully grown. Was he estranged from his family? Were they dead? There weren't even any trophies of war. Maybe he had a secret vault somewhere with all that personal stuff.

The thought should have made her smile, but instead she shuddered as if brushed by a chill. Again the question came to her mind. Who was Jeff?

Ashley shook her head. She decided she didn't

want or need an answer. She wasn't looking for a man in her life, and if she was, Jeff wouldn't make the final cut. While he was efficient, thorough and even kind, he wasn't warm and loving. She was only interested in someone who would love her with body, heart and soul. She wasn't even sure Jeff had a soul.

Which meant she should be grateful for his hospitality and should stop analyzing the man. After all, if he let her stay until her apartment was ready, it meant she could take a minivacation from the trauma that was her life. As her mother used to say, if someone offers you a gift, take it. If you don't like it, you can always exchange it later.

Chapter Five

Ashley spent most of the day studying and sleeping. Around three, the sitter, one of Maggie's preschool teachers, dropped off her daughter.

"Tell me about your day," she said when the sitter had left after refusing payment.

"Cathy read us a whole book and I colored in the number book and we talked about our trip to the zoo next week." Maggie shared the bounty of her experiences over a tuna sandwich.

Ashley listened with half an ear, all the while trying to figure out how to raise the issue of payment with her host. It was one thing to stay in his house, but it was quite another for him to take financial responsibility for Maggie's child care. It's not as if he were the girl's father. In fact, Damian had never once contributed a penny. She rubbed her temples. Thinking about Damian would only make her sad and frustrate her in equal measures, so she wouldn't. And she vowed to talk to Jeff later about him paying for things that he shouldn't.

Maggie swallowed her mouthful of food. "Mommy, are you coming with us to the zoo?" her daughter asked. "Cathy said we need extra grown-ups and I couldn't 'member if you have school."

Blue eyes stared beseechingly. Ashley couldn't help smiling, then touching her daughter's cheek. "I don't have classes, and if Cathy needs help I would be delighted to come along. I love seeing all the animals at the zoo."

"Do they gots kittens?"

"Maybe some really big ones."

"I wish Uncle Jeff had kittens."

"I know you do, sweetie, but he doesn't." She hesitated, not sure how to find out if her daughter was comfortable without scaring her by the question. "Do you miss our apartment?"

"A little."

Maggie drank her milk. The clips Jeff had put in her hair that morning were still crooked. Still, it had been very sweet of him to try.

"I like staying here with Uncle Jeff," Maggie volunteered. "He's very nice." She gave her mother an innocent smile. "Uncle Jeff likes cake. We could make him one."

Ashley couldn't help wondering how much her daughter's generosity had to do with her own affection for the dessert. Although baking something would be a nice gesture, a small thank-you for his kindnesses. She could even make dinner. Her car had been delivered earlier that afternoon. They could make a quick trip to the store and get everything they'd need.

"You know, munchkin," she said, lifting her daughter down from her chair and tapping the tip of her nose, "that's a very good idea. Let me call Jeff's office and see what time he's going to be home. Then we can make a special cake and a special dinner for him."

She found the business card he'd left her and called his office. When she was put through to Brenda, she asked his assistant what time he would be heading home. Brenda put her on hold while she checked with him. As Ashley listened to the soft music, she had the sudden thought that this was all too weird. Would he think she was cooking for him to capture his interest? The way to a man's heart and all that?

Heat flared on her cheeks. She longed to hang up, but it was too late for that. Brenda already knew it was her on the line. She would have to say that she was offering a thank-you and nothing more.

"He said he'll be home at six-thirty," Brenda announced cheerfully.

"Ah, thanks." Ashley wanted to explain but doubted Jeff's assistant cared one way or the other. She hung up and started her shopping list. She would make sure that Jeff understood everything when he got home.

The chocolate cake turned out perfectly. Maggie insisted on helping with the frosting, which meant there were uneven patches and more sticky chocolate on her arms and face than on the cake itself. Ashley had settled on meat loaf for dinner. It was easy and something most people liked. Plus she had a limited supply of cash that wasn't going to cover anything expensive, such as steaks.

She checked the potatoes and steaming green beans, then glanced at the clock. Jeff was due any second.

"Just enough time to get you cleaned up, young lady," she said, taking the rubber spatula from her daughter's hand and urging her toward the sink.

Just then Ashley heard the door to the garage open. Unexpectedly her heart rate doubled and her throat seemed to close up a little.

His footsteps sounded on the wood floor. She froze in the center of the kitchen, not sure if she should dash for cover or brazenly stand her ground and greet him. The confusion didn't make any sense. Why was she suddenly nervous? Nothing had changed.

Jeff entered the kitchen. He glanced at the pots on the stove, at the cake, then looked at Maggie, covered in chocolate frosting and grinning.

"We made you a surprise," the four-year-old announced.

"I can see that," he told her, and turned his attention to Ashley. "How do you feel?"

She swallowed. It was as if he could see through to her soul, she thought, wondering if she would melt under the intensity of his attention. Heat flared again, but this time it wasn't just on her face. Instead her entire body felt hot. As if she'd just stepped into a sauna.

"Better, thanks," she said, hoping her voice sounded more steady than *she* felt. "I, ah, slept a lot, and studied. The worst of the virus is over.'' She forced herself to smile, then motioned to the stove. ''I made dinner.''

''You said you were going to when you called Brenda.''

She ducked her head. ''Yes, well, I didn't think before I called. I'm sorry. That was really dumb.''

''Why?''

She glanced at him from under her lashes. She had a sudden awareness of him as a man. Had his shoulders always been that broad? Why hadn't she noticed before? Was it her illness? Had the flu blunted his effect on her, and if so, how could she get immunized against Jeff Ritter's appeal?

''Ashley?''

She blinked. Oh. He asked her a question. Yeah. Dinner. Why cooking it was dumb. ''I didn't want you to feel obligated to come home.''

One corner of his mouth quirked up. ''I live here.''

''I know that. I meant for dinner. You might have plans, or not want to eat with us. The cake was Maggie's idea.'' She glanced down at her daughter and saw that her four-year-old was following the conversation with undisguised interest.

He smiled at the girl. ''It's a beautiful cake. Thank you.''

Maggie brightened. ''It's really good. Mommy won't let me eat the batter 'cause of eggs, but I licked the frosting and it's perfect.''

''Good.'' He looked back at her. ''So what's for dinner?''

''Meat loaf. Mashed potatoes and gravy. Green beans.''

''Sounds great. Let me go wash up and I'll join you.''

''You will?''

''Unless you don't want me to.''

She forced herself to take a deep breath. ''No. It would be nice to have you eat with us. Really.''

He nodded and left the room. Ashley groaned softly. When had she turned into an idiot? Just this morning she'd had a completely normal conversation with the man. Now she was acting like a freshman with a crush on the football captain. She'd lost her mind, and if she wanted to act like a mature adult, she was going to have to find it again, and fast!

Jeff focused on the report in front of him but he couldn't force any of the words to make sense. He would swear that even from half a house away, he could hear laughter drifting down the stairs and into his study. Earlier he'd heard running water as Ashley prepared her daughter's bath. The nightly routine was as foreign to him as life on another planet, and yet observing it from a distance made him ache inside.

He wanted with a power that nearly drove him to his knees, yet he couldn't for the life of him say *what* he wanted. Connection had never been his strength. Hadn't Nicole told him that dozens of times before she'd left him? Hadn't she hurled the accusation across nearly every argument they'd had? That he'd changed, that he wasn't the man she'd married, that he didn't belong?

And he hadn't belonged with her. In the end, nothing about their life together had been able to touch him. It had been easy when she'd walked away. Or so he'd thought until tonight. Until the laughter of a child and her mother made him wonder what it would have been like if things had been different. If *he'd* been different.

An ache formed inside of him. Deep and dark, it filled him until he couldn't breathe without the emptiness threatening to suck him into a void. He gripped the edge of his desk so tightly, he thought he might snap the sturdy wood...or perhaps a bone in his fingers.

"Uncle Jeff?"

The soft voice made him look up. Maggie stood in the entrance to his study. She wore a pink nightgown under a purple robe. Snowball held the place of honor in her arms. The little girl was freshly scrubbed from her bath, her curls fluffed around her face.

Uncle Jeff. He'd offered that as a substitute for "Mr. Ritter," which had seemed too formal for their present circumstances. Now he questioned the wisdom of claiming a connection where none existed. She would get the wrong idea. Or perhaps it was himself he had to worry about. Perhaps he would be the one to presume affection where there wasn't any. He must never forget who and what he was.

"Are you ready for bed?" he asked, forcing himself to smile at her as if nothing was wrong.

Ashley stepped into the doorway, her hand resting on her daughter's shoulder. "Sorry to disturb you, but she wanted to say good-night."

"Neither of you are interrupting. Sleep well, Maggie."

She bounced free of her mother's restraining hand and raced over to where he sat. Before he knew what she was about, she flung her little arms around his neck and squeezed tight.

She smelled of baby shampoo and honey-scented soap. She was warm and small and so damn trusting. Awkwardly he hugged her back, trying not to press too hard or frighten her in any way. She released him and beamed, then scurried from the room. Ashley lingered.

"Do you mind if we talk for a second?" she said. "After I get her in bed."

"Whenever you'd like."

He tried not to notice how the heat from the bath had flushed her face, nor the way her sweater hugged her feminine curves. He doubted she had all her energy back, but she no longer looked sick.

"Thanks. Give me about fifteen minutes." She turned and left.

Desire filled him. Desire and sexual need. They were both primal and difficult to dismiss. Most of the time he could use work to distract himself from a difficult situation. But not with Ashley. She haunted his thoughts at the office and at his house when he was home. He couldn't forget about her when she walked the halls of the house, leaving proof of her presence in a sound, a scent, a discarded sweater or an open textbook. He had no place to retreat.

However, time and practice had taught him that bodily needs were easily controlled. He'd learned to function without sleep, food or water, while in pain, under stress or physically compromised. Surely he could figure out a way to survive the presence of one woman, regardless of how much she appealed to him. If nothing else, imagining her horror when she figured out the truth about him would be enough to keep his thoughts and actions under control.

Ashley forced herself to take a deep breath before entering Jeff's study. Her sudden attraction to him hadn't gone away over dinner. The only thing she could figure was that she'd been so sick when she'd first met him that she hadn't noticed the appeal of the man or her own weakness where he was concerned. Now that the virus was under control, she was able to feel the pull. Which made for a great science experiment, but didn't help her current situation: how to get through a conversation with him and not act like an idiot.

Practice, she thought desperately. Maybe this was a case of practice making perfect. That decided, or at least hoped for, she tapped on Jeff's open door and walked into his study.

The room was large, with beautiful bookcases on two walls and a bay window on the third wall, overlooking the garden. His wood desk was big enough to double as an extra bed, and two leather club chairs faced the imposing barrier.

Jeff looked up as she entered. He was still wearing his suit, although he'd taken off the jacket and loosened his tie. A few strands of hair fell across his forehead. They should have softened his appearance, but he was as formidable as always.

"Have a seat," he said, motioning to one of the empty club chairs.

She sank into the dark brown leather seat and tried to relax. She had an agenda and a purpose. She would do well to remember both and not think about how his gray eyes made her think of the sea during a storm or the way his long, strong fingers had looked as he briefly touched her daughter's hair. She wasn't sure if he was a kind man, but he was capable of kind acts. Did that make him any safer for her?

"You've been very good to us," she said, plunging in when it became apparent he wasn't going to speak first, which made sense—she'd been the one to request the meeting. "Putting us up, arranging for Maggie to get to school. It's not that I'm not grateful, it's just that there are some things I need to do myself."

He rose. "Are you taking any medication?"

She blinked at him. "What?"

"Are you taking anything for the flu? I was going to offer you a brandy."

"Oh. No. I'm feeling much better. A brandy would be nice."

It would also give her something to hold so she wouldn't have to worry about her fingers twisting together the way they were now.

He opened the doors of a cabinet built into one of the bookcases and withdrew a bottle of brandy along with two glasses.

"Go on with what you were saying. You need to be responsible for some things yourself. Can you be more specific?"

As he spoke, he poured, then handed her a glass. She took it, careful to keep her fingers from touching his. "Thanks. I was talking about the baby-sitter. When she dropped off Maggie she wouldn't let me pay her. That's not right."

He poured his own drink, then settled on a corner of the desk. Which meant he was closer to her than he'd been before. Which meant her heart had jumped into her throat, making it impossible to breathe or swallow.

"You have a point," he said.

"I do?"

He nodded.

She forced herself to be calm. Slowly she found herself breathing again. She even managed to take a tiny sip of the brandy. It was hot and wonderful as it burned its way down to her stomach.

"I didn't mean to take over your life," he said. "I'll give you an invoice for the baby-sitting expenses to date and you can reimburse me."

"I, ah, thank you," she said, surprised he'd seen her side so easily. She also wondered how many times she'd thanked the man since meeting him.

"Anything else?"

As in, did she want to talk about anything else, she supposed. She studied him, thinking that despite the beautiful home and the successful business, he was incredibly alone. Before she and Maggie arrived, there hadn't even been any food in the house. She sensed he lived for work and little else and found herself wondering why.

Of course there could be women, she reminded herself. Maybe it was her own wishful thinking that he spent a lot of time by himself. There could be dozens of girlfriends. But only the kind he didn't invite home, she thought. The house was too silent. There were no echoes of past voices and laughter.

"Ashley?"

"Huh? Oh, sorry. I was lost in thought."

"Want to tell me about what?"

"Not especially." She gave him a false smile, then said the first thing that popped into her mind. "I'm not a widow."

A slight raising of his left eyebrow was his only response.

She closed her eyes and wondered if that had sounded as stupid as she thought. "What I mean is that based on what I said before you probably think I'm a widow, and I'm not. Well, technically Damian is dead, but we divorced first. He died a few months later."

"All right."

She could see he was wondering what possible relevance that information had for him. "It's just that we'd talked about it before. Actually, Maggie mentioned it. She made it sound as if...well..." She cleared her throat and took another sip of her brandy.

"I, ah, should go now," she said, rising to her feet. "You have work and I—"

"You're welcome to stay," he said. "If you're feeling up to a little conversation."

"I—yes, that would be nice." She plopped back onto the seat and smiled. The man made her nervous, but with a little effort on her part, she was sure she could act fairly normal.

"Tell me about school," he said, moving around the desk and settling into his leather executive chair. "Why accounting?"

"It suits me," she said, consciously relaxing in her chair. "I've always enjoyed math and I'm basically an orderly person. I wanted a career that gave me flexibility with my time and didn't tie me down to a big city."

"You want to leave Seattle?"

"No, but I want the option in case that changes."

"Makes sense."

"I started college right out of high school, but with getting married and then getting pregnant, I wasn't able to finish as quickly as I would like."

"But you didn't give up."

He wasn't asking a question. His gray eyes seemed to see past her facade of quiet confidence—if that's what her facade was projecting.

"I'm not the giving-up kind," she admitted, and took another sip of her brandy.

Around them, the night was still. It wasn't raining and there wasn't any wind. In the distance she heard the faint sound of a car, but nothing else. While she and Jeff weren't the only people left in the world, there was an air of solitude in the study. As if they might be cut off from civilization. Oddly, that didn't seem like such a bad thing.

"Who taught you not to quit?" he asked.

She considered the question. "I didn't have a choice. If I'd given up, I wouldn't have survived."

"Why?"

She hesitated, not sure she was ready, or willing, to tell her life story to a virtual stranger. But, despite his emotional distance, Jeff was easy to talk to. Probably because she doubted she could say anything that would shock him. He'd seen and done so much more than she could ever imagine. Her life would be very small in comparison.

"I had a sister who was four years older than me. Margaret…Maggie. I adored her. My dad ran off before I was born, so it was just us three girls. At least that's what my mom used to say.'' She smiled sadly at the memory. ''Mom worked really long hours. She was a waitress. She tried going back to school so she could do something else, but she couldn't make it. She was always so tired. She kept saying that she should have done it when she was young and that we should learn from her mistakes. Don't give up on college no matter what.''

''You took her words to heart.''

Ashley nodded. ''They made a lot of sense.''

He continued to study her. Was he taking her measure? Did he find her wanting? Lamplight touched his hair, illuminating the light strands. There wasn't any gold glinting there—just pure blond. A muscle twitched in his cheek.

''You told me you don't have any family,'' he said. ''Where are they now?''

Involuntarily she looked away, lowering her chin and biting her bottom lip. ''Gone,'' she said softly. ''Maggie was hit by a drunk driver when she was just sixteen. She and a couple of friends were walking home from the library. It was about nine in the evening and they'd been studying for midterms. All three girls were killed instantly.'' She hesitated. ''It was a difficult time.''

The simple sentence didn't begin to explain what she'd gone through. The shock—the incredible pain and disbelief. Her sister, her best friend, was gone.

She clutched the brandy glass in both hands. ''Mom was never the same. She sort of disappeared into herself after that. A few months after Maggie died, Social Services put me in a foster home and my mom in a mental institution. One of the times they let her out for a weekend to visit with me, she killed herself.''

Jeff didn't say anything. Ashley figured there wasn't all that much to say. She'd had more than her share of tragedy. Most of the time she was able to deal with it, but other times it threatened to drag her down.

"What happened after that?" he asked.

She shrugged. "I grew up in a series of foster homes. Most of them were pretty okay. The people tried to be nice and help me fit in. I had some counseling. I managed to make friends and keep up my grades. Unfortunately I had lousy taste in men. I had a series of loser boyfriends. They weren't mean—they just didn't get anything right.''

"Including Damian?"

Ashley tried to remember the last time she'd talked about her past. She usually didn't say anything because there was no way to talk about it without making her life sound like a badly written soap opera. Now she found herself spilling her guts and she couldn't figure out why. She wasn't sure Jeff was even interested.

"Damian tried," she said. "But he wasn't what I wanted him to be. We met during my senior year of high school and I was so sure he was the one. I believed that he would love me unconditionally and forever.''

"Is that what you wanted?"

The question startled her. "Of course. Doesn't everyone?"

"No," he said evenly.

Ashley stared in surprise. Who wouldn't want more

love in their life? She thought about Jeff. He was a man who spent his life alone. Most likely by choice. But why?

She thought about asking, but she wasn't feeling that brave.

"Damian tried," she continued, picking up the thread of her story. "He cared about me, but he was too young and too much of a dreamer. He would rather scheme than work. He was always going to find the pot of gold at the end of the rainbow. Unfortunately his dreams weren't practical, and when it came time to put food on the table, he took shortcuts. I don't know everything he was involved in, but I suspect it was all illegal. By the time I'd figured that out, we were married and I was pregnant. After Maggie was born, I told Damian he was going to have to change his ways or it would be over. It had been scary enough when it was just me, but with a child to consider—" she shook her head "—I couldn't do it."

She wondered if he would ask for details. She didn't want to talk about the strange men who had come to the house in the middle of the night, or the gun she'd found in her husband's coat pocket.

But Jeff didn't ask about that. Instead he said, "When he wouldn't go straight, you left him?"

"I didn't have a choice. I filed for divorce. Six months after it was final, he was killed in a car accident."

"You've been on your own ever since."

Again, not a question.

She nodded.

He leaned forward and set his drink on the desk. "You're strong, Ashley. You've more than survived all that life has handed you—you've succeeded. Not many people can say that.''

His kind words made her squirm. ''I didn't have a choice. There was Maggie to think of.''

''You named her after your sister.''

''I love them both.'' She cleared her throat. ''And things are looking up. In eighteen months I'll have my degree and I'll be able to get a real accounting job, with good pay. Maggie will be entering kindergarten. A couple of years after that, I'll be able to afford a town house for us. We'll be a regular family.''

She was counting the days until that time. She was tired of watching every penny and stretching them until they snapped like rubber bands. She wanted to be able to buy her daughter pretty clothes and occasional dinners out. She wanted to go to the movies every couple of months and maybe even afford a trip to Disneyland.

That would come, she reminded herself. The worst of it was behind her. She would—

''I don't want you going back to work at Ritter/Rankin Security,'' Jeff said.

Her world shattered. In that second, as he spoke those few words, everything changed. Her throat tightened and her hands started to shake.

''Because I brought Maggie to work?'' she asked, barely able to breathe, let alone speak. ''But Jeff, you have to understand why.''

''I do understand. Your schedule is impossible. You don't get any sleep. Your free time is spent studying and taking care of your daughter. You have no savings, no back-up. I'm amazed you've stayed as healthy as you have.''

So why was he firing her? She needed the money and the benefits the job provided. Where else would she get such perfect hours and medical insurance for her child? Her eyes burned, but she refused to give in to the tears.

She set her glass on the desk and rose to her feet. ''You can't fire me,'' she insisted. ''Dammit, Jeff, I do good work. How can you do this—cutting me off without a way to support my child? I'll have to drop out of school. I—''

She couldn't go on. It was so unfair.

''You misunderstand me,'' he told her. ''I'm not trying to make your situation worse. I'm offering you alternative employment. I would like to hire you as my housekeeper. You'll take care of things here— cooking, cleaning, whatever else there is to do. You can live here rent free. In addition, I've spoken with my financial director. There is plenty of contract accounting work. If you're interested, you can do that to supplement your income. The combined amounts should give you about double what you're making now.''

As usual, she couldn't read what he was thinking, but she had a good idea. No doubt he was pleased with himself for acting so magnanimous.

''So I'm your charity case for the month?'' she asked. ''It's an interesting practice, taking people off the street and fixing them. Will you do orphans next?''

''You're overreacting.''

''Probably because I'm a woman, right?'' She

pressed her lips together to hold in the rage. He was playing with her. She didn't understand why, but she recognized the sensation of being manipulated.

"Your offer is generous," she told him. "But I'm not interested. Maggie and I will be fine without you. And we'll be leaving in the morning."

Chapter Six

Ashley hurried to her room. She felt hot and light-headed, as if her flu had returned, but she knew her symptoms weren't that easy to explain. Her eyes burned and her hands balled into fists. She felt angry and embarrassed—but most of all she felt *betrayed*.

How could he have said all that? Offered her all that? It wasn't right. She was a temporary guest in his home and he'd treated her like a—a— She stopped in the center of the upstairs hall and leaned against the wall. She didn't know what he'd treated her like, but it made her feel ugly inside. As if she'd somehow been selling herself. As if... Damn.

Ashley sank onto the floor, pulling her knees up to her chest. Shame flooded her as the truth crashed over her with the subtlety of a Midwestern thunderstorm. She was an idiot. A down-to-the-bones kind of fool.

Jeff Ritter had come out of nowhere and rescued her. There was no other way to describe his taking charge of her life and setting everything right. He'd brought her into his gorgeous home and he'd been kind to her and her daughter. The second the flu bug had departed her system, she'd found out she was incredibly aware of him as a man. She thought he was good-looking and sexually intriguing. That kind of attraction hadn't happened to her in years. In fact she'd been so immune, she'd assumed that part of her was dead.

She'd been startled to feel like a woman again and she'd gone from zero to having-a-crush-on in less than nine seconds. His offers for her to be his house-keeper and do part-time accounting work had blown her fantasy apart in a single breath. She'd been left feeling like an idiot and acting even worse.

It was the stress in her life, she told herself. Too much to do, too little time and money. Years of just getting by had worn her down. At the least little upset, she'd fallen apart. So she'd thought Jeff was the an-swer to a single mom's prayers and he'd thought she was efficient hired help. Did that matter? He wasn't responsible for her fantasies being destroyed. She shouldn't be having them in the first place.

She leaned her head against the wall and wished she could take back the past fifteen minutes and have them to do over again. This time she would see his offer for what it was—kindness from a stranger, not a rejection from a fantasy lover. Unfortunately time wasn't going to bend just for her.

Jeff stared at the chair Ashley had used and won-dered what the hell had happened. Somehow he'd upset her or insulted her, or both. She was going to leave in the morning and he couldn't stop her. Not that he should want to.

He drained the last of his brandy and hoped the fire burning down to his stomach would ease some of the ache inside. He could almost remember a time when normal conversations had been simple. When he'd been comfortable around people and had taken pleasure in their company. He could remember laughing with Nicole. Touching her, kissing her. He remembered easy words spoken without thinking. Not anymore. Not ever. He weighed each word, wondering if he was getting it right. Because he didn't know how to do that anymore.

He'd been so close, too. Ashley had opened up to him, telling him about her past. He knew enough of the world to be able to read what she *didn't* say as much as what she did. He imagined a frightened girl of twelve, losing both her mother and her sister within a few months of each other. A teenager looking for love with boys who were clueless about what that meant.

Somehow she'd survived, saving both herself and her daughter. She'd even kept her humanity—something he hadn't been able to manage.

He thought about how the light had played on her face, illuminating perfect skin, emphasizing wide hazel eyes. Her smile seemed to come from the heart. She was smart and determined, and thin in a way that made him wonder how many times she'd had money to feed her daughter, but not herself.

Sometime that afternoon he'd come up with a plan

to rescue her. He'd worked out the details and then he'd spoken without thinking and he'd insulted her. Because he had a need to fix, to mend. It didn't matter that it wasn't his business or that she wasn't his problem. In an odd and dangerous way, he wanted to be responsible. Which meant that there was something wrong with him. He knew better than to get involved. His soul was too dead to allow for any kind of connection beyond the physical.

Still, he had to make amends. He might not understand the extent of his transgression, but he would do his best to make it right.

He walked through the house to the stairs and climbed to the second floor. He turned toward the guest wing, then paused when he saw Ashley sitting on the floor, leaning against the wall. Faint light from her bedroom spilled into the hallway, illuminating the left side of her face.

Desire rushed through him, making him need with an intensity that sucked the breath from his lungs. She was soft and sweet. Her gentleness called to him. As if he could risk being with someone gentle. As if she wouldn't run in horror if she knew the truth about him, that in the deepest, darkest part of him, he'd ceased to be a man.

She looked up at him and smiled slightly. "I was sitting here trying to talk myself into going back downstairs and apologizing. You've saved me the trip."

Her words didn't make sense. "You have nothing to apologize for."

"What about the fact that I seriously overreacted? That should count for something. You were just being nice and I took it wrong. At least I assume you were being nice.''

Nice? Him? ''I was trying to do the right thing. I need a housekeeper and you need to make a change in your work.''

She wrinkled her nose. ''You do like telling me what to do. Is this a military thing or a male thing?''

''Both.''

''Figures.'' She sighed. ''It's not that I don't appreciate the offer, Jeff.''

''But you don't trust me.''

Her gaze sharpened. ''It's not that exactly.''

But it was that. He could read it in her eyes. She wanted to believe and she wasn't sure. Could he blame her for that?

I want you.

The words remained unspoken, but they burned inside of him. He wanted and he needed with equal intensity. He wanted to inhale the scent of her body, touching her everywhere. He wanted to feel the silk of her short, dark hair and taste her mouth. He wanted to fill her until they both forgot everything but the heat of the moment.

Instead he drew in a slow breath. ''The offer still stands. I hope you'll reconsider.''

''I can't.''

He wanted to ask why. He wanted to know how she'd figured out the truth about him so quickly. How had she learned that the safest course for her was to run away? He wanted to protest her decision, telling her that she was the closest to caring that he'd come in years. That when he was with her and Maggie, sometimes he forgot he wasn't like everyone else.

What he said instead was "Let me know if you change your mind."

And then he walked away, because if he didn't, he would say something he would regret. He might even tell her the truth.

The next morning Ashley carefully replaced the phone in the cradle when what she wanted to do was throw it across the room and stomp her feet. She hadn't thought it was possible for her life to get any worse, but she'd been wrong. One brief sentence had turned her world upside down. Just one sentence.

"Your apartment building has been condemned."

With that, her home was gone. The city official had been very polite, offering assistance in finding a new place to live. However, there were no plans to help her with the costs of moving, nor was she likely to find such low rent. She was completely and totally screwed.

The timing was incredible. Just last night she'd told Jeff they would be moving out in the morning. Mostly because she'd expected her apartment to be habitable by now. Talk about being completely wrong.

She wanted to go back to bed, pull the covers over her head and wait for the world to go away. Unfortunately that wasn't likely to happen. Instead she had a child to worry about, and classes, not to mention solving her living arrangement issue.

She left her bedroom and moved toward the stairs. Smile, she told herself as she walked down the hall. Jeff mustn't know she was in such dire straits and she didn't want Maggie worrying, either.

She stepped into the kitchen to find her daughter

and Jeff having breakfast together. Neither of them looked up, although she was reasonably confident that Jeff knew she'd arrived. She ignored the man sitting at the table and instead focused on her daughter.

She'd dressed Maggie in her favorite pink corduroy overalls with a matching pink-and-white kitten-print shirt. She'd washed her daughter's face, helped her with her shoes and socks, but she hadn't had time to do her hair. Yet Maggie's curls were drawn back from her face with two tiny, plastic, pink barrettes. They weren't even, or anchored to last the day, but they were in place.

There was no way her daughter had managed to fasten them in her hair, which left only one possibility. Ashley's gaze slid to her host. Jeff was in a suit, as usual. In fact she didn't remember seeing him wear anything else. His white shirt was starched, his tie perfectly in place. He was showered, shaven and ready to start his day.

The breadth of his shoulders spoke of his strength. His firm mouth barely smiled. Yet he'd taken the time to fix a little girl's hair. Something he'd done before. Maggie wasn't afraid of him. If anything, she adored Jeff. She'd trusted him from the first moment they'd met. Was that the intuition of a trusting child, or the hunger of a fatherless girl to interact with a substitute male? Ashley knew generalities about Jeff—that he was a former soldier, a dangerous man who excelled in a potentially deadly occupation. But what did she know about the person inside? What was his story?

"Mommy?" Maggie had looked up and seen her in the doorway. "I'm eating all my cereal."

"Good for you." Ashley raised her chin slightly. "Jeff, may I speak to you for a second?"

He nodded and rose to his feet, then joined her in the hallway. "Is there a problem?" he asked.

She stared into gray eyes. She couldn't read him any better than she had when she'd first arrived. "I talked to someone from the city just now. Did you know my apartment building had been condemned?"

His gaze never wavered. "No, but I'm not surprised. The water damage looked extensive."

"I have to find a new apartment."

He folded his arms over his chest. "Do you have the money?"

"No."

She waited for him to pounce—to again make the offer of a job she was going to have to take. Because in some strange way, she was testing him.

"All right. I'll write you a check to cover the costs. Pay me back when you can. After you graduate from college is fine."

Not the offer she'd expected at all. She sagged against the door frame. "Who are you, Jeff?"

"Why does it matter?"

Because he was making her want to believe in him and she'd learned to never believe in anyone but herself. Besides, he couldn't have made it more clear he wasn't the least bit interested in her skinny self.

A knock at the front door interrupted them. Maggie rushed past, eager to greet Brenda. Ashley turned away from Jeff without answering his question and hurried after her daughter.

Brenda was already inside the house and hugging

the little girl. "It's raining this morning," she said. "You're going to need a jacket."

"I know where it is!" Maggie announced, turning around and racing toward the stairs. "I'll get it, Mommy."

"Thank you, sweetie," Ashley called after her, then went to speak with Jeff's assistant.

Brenda smiled at her as she approached. "I know you're feeling better, but I appreciate you letting me take her to school this morning. I just adore her." The older woman sighed. "Grandkids are the best and Maggie is just as sweet as my daughter's little girl."

"You're more than welcome." Ashley glanced over her shoulder to make sure they were still alone, then invited the other woman into the living room. "I need to ask you a question," she said. "It's probably going to sound a little strange and I apologize if it makes you uncomfortable."

Brenda settled on a beige sofa and grinned. "Now I'm wildly intrigued. Go ahead."

Ashley checked again to make sure no one lurked in the hallway, then joined her guest on the couch. "To be blunt, can I trust Jeff? Through an assortment of circumstances, I'm in a difficult situation right now. Jeff has offered me a job as his housekeeper. It would mean living here with my daughter. On the one hand it's a great opportunity. The money is good, the house is terrific. But I don't know him very well and I do have a young child to be concerned about."

"Don't worry about Jeff at all," Brenda said, lightly touching her forearm. "I know he's a little formidable and he doesn't talk about himself, but he's a great guy. I've known him for nearly five years and

I would trust him with my life. Better, I would trust him with my grandkids'.''

Which was what Ashley needed to know. ''Thanks for telling me.''

Brenda tilted her head slightly, then tucked a strand of blond hair behind her ear. ''At the risk of being presumptuous, I do have one more thing to say.''

''Which is?''

''He's not a people person, so don't expect witty banter. And he's very solitary. As far as I know, he hasn't had a serious relationship in the past five years. So don't even think about giving away your heart.''

Ashley smiled. ''Not a problem. I'm not interested in getting involved.''

While she might find the man sexy and appealing on a physical level, emotionally she knew better than to risk her feelings again. If she ever did that again, it was going to be with someone who could love her more than anyone else in the world.

''Then you should be just fine.''

Maggie burst into the living room. She had her jacket dragging from one arm and her backpack trailing from the other. ''I'm ready,'' she announced.

Ashley laughed. ''Not exactly, young lady. Come here.''

In less than five minutes, Maggie was ready to leave for school. Ashley kissed her goodbye and promised to pick her up promptly at two. Brenda gave her a quick wave and a thumbs-up, then they left. Ashley was alone with Jeff. It was decision time.

She found him in his office, packing his briefcase. Had he worked into the night? she wondered. She hadn't been able to sleep much, mostly because she'd been thinking about his offer and how badly she'd acted. What had kept him up through the long dark hours?

She knocked on the open door, then stepped inside. "Do you have a minute?"

"Of course."

He motioned for her to take one of the seats in front of his desk. She did, choosing the one she hadn't sat in the night before. He relaxed into his chair.

She licked her lips. "I want to ask if your offer is still open."

"For the loan?"

"No. The job."

He raised his eyebrows and nodded instead of speaking.

Good. At least she hadn't blown it so much that he'd changed his mind.

"I'm interested," she told him. "But I need to know why you're bothering. You could get someone in here a couple of times a week to do the cooking and cleaning. Why a full-time live-in housekeeper and why me?"

He didn't answer right away. Instead he seemed to consider the question. Which made her squirm in her seat. Was she being inappropriate with her questions? Would he get angry? Did she want to work for him if his temper had such a short fuse?

"I know you well enough to trust you in my house," he said at last. "Besides, I like your daughter."

Her nerves were frayed. One snapped. "Then have a couple of kids of your own."

Thoughtful gray eyes turned toward her. "I can't."

She'd been expecting half a dozen answers, but not that one. "I don't understand."

"I have a low sperm count. It makes conception highly unlikely."

She blinked. Her mind seemed to sway slightly as a couple hundred questions formed in her mind. How had he known? That wasn't the sort of information one learned in a routine examination. He had to have been tested for fertility. Which meant what? That he'd been trying to get someone pregnant at one time? So at one time...

"You were married?"

A slight smile tugged at the corners of his mouth. "I know that's hard to believe."

"No, it's not that."

Although it was. She couldn't imagine Jeff on bended knee, proposing. And married? As in living with a woman? Being casual in jeans, maybe, or walking around unshaven, wearing a robe? It boggled the mind.

"I was married for several years. We tried to have children. When she didn't get pregnant, we were both tested. The fault was mine."

Was that why he wasn't married anymore? Was that— She realized that it was none of her business. "I'm sorry," she murmured. "I didn't mean to pry."

"I understand your concern. While I like Maggie, I don't think of her as a substitute daughter."

He picked up a pen and studied it. On anyone else, Ashley would swear the action was a stall for time. Finally he set the pen down.

"I don't make a habit of being a nice guy, which is why I'm doing this so badly," he said. "You work for me. I have no intention of firing you. If you want a loan for relocating to another apartment and your old job back, you're welcome to both. If you'd like to try being my housekeeper on a trial basis, that's fine, too. I don't want anything from you or your daughter.'' He paused. Something dark passed across his face. ''If you're looking for an explanation for my actions, think of them as atonement.''

''For what?''

He shrugged. ''I'm damn good at what I do. I was better as a soldier. That comes with a price.''

She didn't want to ask anymore because she didn't want to know what he'd done. She remembered the article that mentioned his time in Special Ops. There were hints about covert assignments. Assassinations. Secret battles.

He was dangerous. She knew that in her head, but she couldn't feel it in her heart. As if she was exempt from the ruthlessness. Was that possible?

''I have a small child,'' she said. ''Considering your line of work, I'm assuming you have guns in the house. Will she be safe?''

Instead of answering in words, he rose to his feet. At the far end of the room, he touched a book on a shelf and the entire bookcase swung open. Ashley rose and followed him. He pointed to the large safe built into the wall.

''There's no key or combination lock. It requires a retinal scan. The mechanism has its own power source so it won't be disabled by an electrical blackout. Everything dangerous is kept in there.''

She thought about asking what all might be in inventory, but figured she was better off not knowing.

"Maggie is perfectly safe," he said. "I wouldn't let her stay here otherwise."

Ashley shivered. She wanted reassurance that she would be safe, too.

"I'd like the housekeeper job," she said, shoving her hands into her jeans pockets and taking a step back. "Just for a couple months, until I get my feet under me."

"Fair enough." He closed the bookcase. "Are you interested in the accounting work, as well?"

In for a penny, as they say. "Yes."

"Good."

He stared at her. Something flickered against his irises. For a second she would have sworn she saw fire—the kind that burned bright from passion's desire. If he had been any other man, she would have thought he was interested. But not Jeff. Certainly not in her.

Chapter Seven

It took Ashley less than forty-eight hours to invade his world. Jeff had always had a biweekly cleaning service that took care of the house and washed his sheets and towels, but now he had a *housekeeper*.

Ashley took her work seriously. Pieces of furniture that had simply been dusted were now polished. Surfaces gleamed and the scent of lemon filled the air. He found vases of flowers on tables and light filtering in through sparkling windows. His sheets and towels were softer, his cupboards stocked with food and meals had become multi-course and nutritional. When he gave her accounting work, she did it quickly and accurately, returning it to him the following day.

Jeff hadn't realized how careful she'd been to keep to herself while she was simply a guest in his house. Now her presence was everywhere. Her perfume lingered in the hallway. A couple of Maggie's toys found their way to the family room. Schoolbooks stacked up on an end table. It was as if a family lived here.

A family. The concept was unfamiliar. He knew intellectually that there had been a time when he'd belonged to a family. He'd been born to parents who lived in suburbs, just like regular people. Jeff knew he'd been a part of that world once—playing sports in high school, hanging out with his friends. But those memories weren't real to him. It was as if he'd seen a movie about someone's past. A past that happened to be his own. He couldn't relate to those images and he didn't know how to act now that he was no longer alone.

He glanced at his watch. It was late, nearly midnight. Maggie was long asleep, but Ashley was still up, studying in the kitchen. The need to go to her compelled him to rise to his feet, even though he knew he shouldn't bother her. He walked toward the light, knowing he had no right to want to be with her, even when all he expected was simple conversation.

She haunted him. Much like the ghosts of his past, she was a constant presence in his mind. Yet unlike the memories of the dead, she made him feel better for occupying his thoughts. She made him anticipate—something he hadn't done in years. She made him need, which reminded him he was alive. But was that good or bad?

He reached the kitchen and stood in the doorway. The overhead light glinted off her dark hair. She wore jeans and a sweater. Her feet were bare and she'd tucked one up under her on the straight-backed chair.

Several books lay open across the table. She glanced at one, then returned her attention to the accounting paper in front of her.

One curl caressed her cheek. Looking at it made him press his fingers into his palm. He wanted to touch the curl...and the cheek. He wanted to feel the silk of her skin and the warmth of her body. He wanted...

"Are you just going to stand there, or are you going to join me?" She spoke without looking up.

Jeff frowned. He knew he hadn't made any noise. "How did you know I was here?"

She glanced at him and smiled. "It's a mom thing. Internal radar. The same mechanism tells me when Maggie is doing something she shouldn't." She pushed her foot against the chair next to her, moving the seat toward him in invitation. "I'm due to take a break." She pointed at the closest open textbook. "It's cost accounting, so you're doing me a favor by taking me away from it for a while. There are fresh cookies. Want one?"

He followed the direction of her finger and saw a heaping plate of cookies on the counter. "You're always trying to feed me."

She smiled. "That's because you don't eat very much. I'm a compulsive feeder."

"Another mom thing?"

"Probably. I want to take care of the world."

He moved toward the table, but didn't take the seat next to her. Instead he settled across from her—as much to see her as to make sure he wasn't close enough to touch. Something about the late hour made him question his ability to do the right thing. The need inside seemed to grow with each tick of the kitchen clock.

"Not all mothers are compelled to take care of everyone," he said. "It's about being a giver more than being maternal."

"Maybe." She rose to her feet and walked over to the cookie plate. After moving a couple of her books, she set it in the center of the table, then headed to the refrigerator. "What about your mother? What was she like?"

"A homemaker," he said as Ashley poured them each a glass of milk. "She liked to sew and bake. My dad worked for Ford. On the assembly line."

She put a full glass in front of him and resumed her seat. "Let me guess. You played football and were something of a flirt."

"I'll admit to the football."

Ashley had been kidding when she'd asked the question. She couldn't imagine Jeff as a young man. She'd never seen him out of a suit. Even now, despite the late hour, he wore a white shirt and slacks. He'd discarded his tie and rolled up his sleeves, but he hadn't bothered changing into something more casual. Did the man own jeans?

Not that it mattered. She was glad she had the cookies and milk to give her something other than Jeff to look at and touch. Otherwise she wasn't sure she could control herself around him. She'd never once in her life wanted to be sick, but right now she couldn't help wishing for a bit of the flu bug to return because it seemed to be the only thing that kept her immune to Jeff's masculine charms.

She hated the way she noticed the strength in his

hands and wrists and the shivery sensation in her belly as she studied the stubble darkening his jaw. His voice sent ripples of need dancing along her spine and the darkness of the night made her think of bed and tangled sheets. She tried to convince herself it was a lack of male companionship that made her overreact to her new boss, but she was afraid it wasn't that simple. Something chemical happened when she was around the man and she didn't know how to make it stop.

Conversation, she told herself as her breathing increased slightly. Talk about something normal and maybe he won't notice the sexual tension in the air.

"What sent you into the army?" she asked.

"I didn't want to go to college. I liked sports, but I wasn't a big fan of school. I wanted to see the world."

"Did you?"

He picked up a cookie. "I saw a lot of places I didn't want to see."

"Is that where you met your wife?"

He bit into the cookie and chewed. "No. She and I had dated in high school. We married right before I enlisted."

It sounded so normal. A guy marrying his high school sweetheart. Ashley looked at Jeff and frowned. She couldn't imagine a moment of it. "You two were pretty young," she said.

"Agreed. Too young. I'd signed up for four years. From day one I knew I'd found where I belonged. I was sent into special operations almost right away. Nicole and I had thought we would be together after boot camp, but that didn't happen. They didn't allow dependents in the places I went, so we were apart more than we were together. That was hard on both of us.''

''Marriage is difficult under the best of circumstances,'' she pointed out, trying not to notice the intimacy of the night. The overhead light illuminated the table, but the rest of the kitchen was in shadows. Outside, the darkness was silent. There weren't even any cars driving by.

''Things changed,'' he said. ''I had assignments that were...'' He hesitated as if searching for the right word. ''Challenging. I couldn't talk about most of what I did, and what I could talk about she didn't want to hear. After a while we stopped talking.''

Ashley knew he'd seen things she couldn't even imagine. There were horrors in the world that no sane person would want to know about. But what of the people who had no choice but to live through those experiences?

''You changed,'' Ashley said, making a statement rather than asking a question.

His gaze sharpened. ''That's what Nicole said.''

''Wasn't she telling the truth? How could those circumstances not change you?''

''You're right.'' He stared into the distance, as if exploring his past. ''In the end she decided it was easier to leave than to make the marriage work.''

''Do you regret that?''

''No.''

She wondered if he was telling the truth. ''Accepting that a relationship isn't going to work is really tough,'' she said, then nibbled on a cookie. ''I had to make that decision when I was married to Damian.

When it was just the two of us, his irresponsibility didn't seem like such a big deal, but after Maggie was born, it mattered more.''

She sipped her milk. ''Some of the reason I resisted the truth was that I didn't want to admit that I'd made a wrong decision. I'd been so sure he was the one. But within the first couple of months, I knew he wasn't. Still, I tried to fix him. I tried to make him see that working hard at a good job was better than all his dreams about getting rich quick. I wanted the marriage to work.''

''Wanting isn't always enough.''

She sighed. ''I learned that one in spades. Finally I saw that the only person I could save was myself. Damian was getting involved in some scary stuff. I couldn't risk that. I had a daughter to take care of. So I left and hoped he would save himself.''

She stared at the table, then began pushing around the cookie crumbs. ''It's like with my mom. After my sister was killed, Mom just lost it. Physically she was in the room, but her mind was somewhere else. I begged her to stay with me, to get better, but I couldn't fix her or save her.''

Her throat tightened. She didn't usually allow herself to think about her past—certainly not the time when she lost both her sister and her mother, albeit in different ways.

''You're strong,'' Jeff told her. ''A lot of people would have cracked under the pressure, but you survived. That's admirable. You kept your head and your sense of humor.''

His praise made her flush. ''Yeah, well, sometimes that's all I did have. At least until Maggie. Now she keeps me focused on what's important. As long as we're together we'll be fine.''

"Your daughter is very lucky. I respect you, Ashley. I know this has been a difficult time for you. I won't do anything to betray your trust in me.''

She looked up and met his steady gaze. Suddenly the room was filled with crackling electricity. She felt mesmerized and incapable of thinking for herself.

Jeff stood. Involuntarily she found herself doing the same. Her chest was tight. Her fingers began to tremble. As he moved around the table, she knew with a certainty that she couldn't explain that he was going to kiss her. Right there in the kitchen. Her heart thundered, her breath came in gasps. Anticipation filled her as her breasts seemed to swell and that secret place between her legs grew damp.

Now, she thought desperately as he got closer. The world around them faded. There was only the night and the man.

They stood less than a foot apart. She kept herself from reaching for him because she desperately wanted him to touch her first. She knew how it would be between them. An explosion. There would be nothing subtle or gentle, but she found she didn't mind that.

"Good night, Ashley," he murmured, and then he was gone.

Her lips parted and she gasped a protest, but it was too late. As quickly as it had blossomed to life, the moment died, leaving her feeling cold and incredibly alone.

Had she been wrong? Hadn't he planned to kiss her? She would have sworn he'd been thinking about it as much as she had. Yet he'd resisted.

She wanted to run after him. She wanted to follow him and beg him to take her, to say that they didn't need promises or commitments. She would accept just the moment and expect nothing more. Instead she sank onto her chair and closed her eyes.

She was a single mother—she couldn't afford to live for moments. She had to be responsible. Whatever insanity caused her to think such thoughts about Jeff had to be ignored. Did she really plan to have sex with her boss? Talk about stupid. She was staying in the man's house.

She sucked in a deep breath and forced herself to resume her studying. She had a lot of work to get through before she could go to bed, and the alarm would go off very early. But instead of numbers and text, she saw Jeff's gray eyes. She remembered the fire she'd seen burning there and wondered how she'd ever thought his eyes were cold.

Ashley hovered outside of Jeff's at-home office. She didn't like to think of herself as a person who hovered, but no other word fit. Except maybe *lurked* and she liked that choice even less.

It's not that she'd been avoiding him in the past couple of days. Okay, maybe she hadn't exactly been around as much, but that was mostly because the kiss-that-had-never-happened had left her feeling embarrassed and stupid. She'd been thinking warm, fuzzy thoughts about Jeff and he'd been thinking less than nothing about her.

So in an effort to keep herself from making a complete idiot of herself, not to mention losing a great job, she'd stayed out of his way. Until now, when she was hovering and trying to gather the courage to step into his office and just ask him.

Finally she simply sucked in a breath and stepped into the study. It was early—only a few minutes after seven in the morning—but Jeff was already showered and dressed for the office. He was putting several folders into his briefcase, which made her wonder how late he'd been working the previous night and did the man actually sleep?

He looked up at her and gave her a slight smile. "Good morning. What can I do for you?"

She thought of about a dozen things, most of which had nothing to do with her reason for being in his office and everything to do with the large bed in his room and the soft feel of bare skin on sheets.

She had to clear her throat to speak. "It's...um—" Her voice failed. What was she doing here? There was no way Jeff would even consider doing this.

"Ashley?"

She sighed. Idiot or not, she was going to have to ask. "I spoke to Cathy, at Maggie's school. Today is their field trip to the zoo and they're short a couple of parents. I'm already going, but Cathy asked if I knew anyone else who would be interested in accompanying the kids and I thought maybe..." She pressed her lips together and stared at the carpet. "You like Maggie and, well, it was a stupid idea."

"Are you inviting me along?"

She nodded then forced herself to meet his gaze. What was he thinking? Please God, don't let him be able to see her uncontrollable and growing attraction. That would be too humiliating to bear.

"Cathy likes to have one adult for every couple of

kids, so if you went, we'd be responsible for four. One of them would be Maggie, of course.''

''You'd stay with me?'' he asked. ''I wouldn't have to be alone with the children?''

She couldn't help grinning. ''Jeff, they don't bite.''

''Sometimes they do.'' He closed his briefcase. ''I'd be happy to come along. Give me ten minutes to call the office and leave Brenda a message, then change my clothes.''

''Sure. Great.''

She backed out of the office before he could sense the elation that swept through her. He was joining her. They would spend the entire day together. Okay, they would have four rug rats with them and this was more about Maggie than her, but still. A shiver of pleasure rippled through her.

Ten minutes later Jeff walked down the stairs. Ashley was busy helping Maggie into her coat, which meant she was kneeling on the floor. A good thing because she probably would have fallen over if she'd been standing.

He'd changed his clothes. Nothing unusual in that. People did it all the time. But she'd never seen Jeff in anything but a suit, and in jeans and a sweater he was gorgeous. Broad shoulders pulled at the woolen fabric. His chest narrowed to his waist, where his jeans emphasized his slim hips. Soft, faded denim clung to thighs as solid and well shaped as a Greek god's.

Maggie squealed when she saw him. ''Mommy said you're comin' with us to the zoo. I wanna see *all* the animals. And baby kitties. And elephants, 'cause next to the kitties, I like them the best. Because of their ears.''

Jeff squatted next to her daughter, which put him way too close to herself. ''Not the trunks?''

Maggie wrinkled her nose. ''Trunks are silly. But they have neat ears.''

Jeff grinned. Ashley's heart froze for a second, before attempting a land speed record in thumps per second. Jeff occasionally joked and he smiled fairly regularly, but he didn't grin much. There were almost dimples in his cheeks and great crinkles by his eyes. If he did that grin thing too much, he could generate enough heat to melt the polar ice caps.

Sensible, she reminded herself as she finished helping Maggie with her coat and rose. She had to be sensible. She wasn't looking for a relationship with a man. She preferred her life to be simple. When she was finally ready to get involved again, she wanted someone who could love her best. She had a feeling that Jeff wasn't in a position to open his heart to anyone. So why go looking for trouble?

''Here you are.''

She turned and saw Jeff holding up her coat for her. As she slipped into it, she accidentally brushed her cheek against his hand. Fire burned from the point of contact. She sighed. It seemed like she wasn't going to have to look for trouble. It was finding her all on its own.

Four-year-olds found everything about the zoo endlessly fascinating. Jeff watched in amazement as his charges raced toward the giraffe exhibit. The kids were as excited by the drinking fountains and benches as they were by the animals.

"What are you thinking?" Ashley asked. "Having second thoughts?"

"Never."

"I'm glad, because you're great with the kids."

He risked glancing at her, taking in the perfect smoothness of her skin and the laughter lurking in her hazel eyes. She was endlessly pretty, he thought, and more than appealing. He was finding it more and more difficult to spend time with her and not give in to his need. He'd come close a couple of times, compelled by a desire that grew so quickly, it was difficult to contain.

When he'd first brought Ashley home, she wanted to know who he was and what he was doing in her world. Now he wanted to ask her the same question. Who was this woman who had made a place for herself in his cold and empty life?

"Jeff, Jeff, pick me up so I can see 'em!"

The instruction came from a blond little boy named Tommy. For reasons that weren't clear to Jeff, the boy had latched on to him from the second they'd been introduced.

Jeff bent awkwardly and lifted the boy in his arms. "There you go."

The slight weight shifted as the kid squirmed to get a better look at the giraffes strolling through their compound.

"Are the elephants next, Mommy?" a familiar voice asked.

"Yes, Maggie. In just a few minutes. Aren't the giraffes pretty, with their long necks?"

Maggie glanced at him as if to say her mother simply wasn't getting it. Cats and elephants were the only animals that interested Maggie.

"Can I touch 'em?" Tommy asked.

Jeff shrugged. "Do you want to keep all your fingers?"

Tommy's blue eyes widened. His hands curled into fists. "They eat fingers?"

"No, but they bite. Animals in the zoo aren't pets. We have to treat them with respect because they're wild creatures."

The boy regarded him solemnly. Tommy had a stain on the front of his flannel shirt and a cowlick that sent a lock of hair up toward the heavens.

"Are you Maggie's daddy?"

The question caught Jeff off guard. He lowered the boy to the ground. "No."

Two of the kids pushed to get closer to the fence, keeping visitors away from the animals. In the process, one of the kids, a girl in pigtails, landed on her butt. Before she more than opened her mouth to scream, one of the mothers pulled her to her feet and distracted her by pointing out the baby giraffe.

Jeff looked at the group of children and parents. They moved and interacted with a grace and rhythm he couldn't understand or copy. He was very much the outsider, but he couldn't decide if he wanted to be anything else.

"Elephants next," Cathy, the preschool teacher called. "Let's go this way."

The children yelped with excitement and hurried after her.

"Not exactly special ops in the jungle, huh?" Ashley said as she stepped next to him. "So, is this more or less challenging than your last security job?"

"It's different."

"Mommy, Uncle Jeff, elephants," Maggie called as she raced past them.

"Don't run, young lady," Ashley instructed. Her daughter slowed marginally.

The late-morning air was cool. There hadn't been any rain in a couple of days and most of the clouds had blown away to the east. Jeff inhaled the scent of the trees and plants around them and tried to ignore the sweet scent that was Ashley alone.

She made him ache with wanting. She made him want to kiss her and touch her, even though he knew he could never do either. Being with her would destroy them both, because she would eventually figure out who and what he was. Then where would they be? Life was easier when he remembered his limitations.

"Why are elephants gray?" one of the boys asked. "Why do they have trunks? Why are they so big? Do they eat people?"

Ashley laughed. "I'll bet we can read all about the elephants when we get there."

The boy wasn't impressed. "Don't you know?"

She turned to Jeff. "What about it, big guy? Want to take the elephant questions?"

"I had to answer questions in the bug house, and that was a lot harder."

"I don't believe you."

They walked toward the re-creation of a tropical forest for the elephants. Other children from a different school were already chattering about the big mammals. Jeff paused to count heads, making sure the entire group was still together. He could—

A sharp cry cut through the morning. Jeff turned and was moving toward the sound before he even understood what he heard. Tommy had fallen and sat cradling his small hand against his chest. As Jeff approached, he saw the child had skinned his palm. Fat tears spilled from his blue eyes.

One of the mothers got there first. She reached for the boy, but Tommy pushed her away. Instead, still crying, he stumbled to his feet and swayed toward Jeff.

"I have disinfectant and stick-on bandages with me," someone said.

Jeff stared as the boy approached. His small body shook with the force of his sobs. Not knowing what else to do, Jeff picked up the child and held him against his chest. Tommy buried his face in Jeff's neck. His tears were hot. The boy hiccupped.

"Let me see," Ashley said softly, gently tugging on the boy's arm so she could free his hand.

Tommy shrieked in protest.

"Come on, big guy," Jeff said, feeling awkward as everyone stared at them. "Let's look over the damage. I'm gonna bet we can fix you right up."

The boy raised his head and sniffed, then held out his hand.

Jeff looked over the wound. It was superficial and barely bleeding. There was a bit of dirt in the scrape, along with a couple of small pebbles.

"It needs washing, disinfectant and a bandage," Ashley pronounced. "Want me to take care of him?"

Jeff wanted nothing more, but at her words Tommy shrieked and wrapped his arms around Jeff's neck.

"I'll do it," he said and took the supplies from one of the mothers. He found a sign pointing toward the rest rooms and headed in that direction.

"We'll wait here for you," Ashley called after him.

"I hate elephants," Tommy murmured. "They're bad."

"But the elephants didn't make you fall. Sometimes we fall all on our own and it's not anyone's fault."

The boy continued to cling to him. Still feeling like an idiot, and as if he was doing everything wrong, Jeff gently touched the boy's shoulder. The child was so small and fragile. He could span the kid's back with his hand. Confusion filled him. What the hell was he doing here? He didn't know how to take care of a child.

But there wasn't anyone else around and Tommy was depending on him. Jeff figured it couldn't be any worse than taking out a bullet or setting a bone in the field. Except emergency care for his team had never made him feel strange inside. As if something was cracking. But what he didn't know was if the ice around his heart was letting go or if his wall of protection was being breached. Or were they the same? And how long would it take to find out if the change was going to destroy him?

Chapter Eight

"But what about the camels that lost their humps?" Maggie asked that night, her eyes wide. "Aren't they sad?"

"Some camels only have one hump. They haven't lost anything. They're just different."

Ashley bit back a smile. After ten minutes of grilling by her daughter, Jeff was still the picture of patience. He put down his fork and leaned toward her daughter.

"Remember the elephants you liked so much? There are two kinds of those, African and Asian elephants. It's the same with camels. Some have one hump and some have two."

They were sitting around the kitchen table at dinner. Ashley tried to ignore how good Jeff looked and the way the meal made her able to think of them as a family. They weren't a family. They barely knew each other. The fact that Jeff had insisted they all eat together was just him being nice.

She frowned. "Nice" didn't exactly describe his actions. Now that she thought about it, why *did* he want to eat with them? Not that she was complaining. Mealtimes were always interesting when he was around.

"Why are camels different?" her daughter asked.

Jeff hesitated, as if forming an answer. Ashley decided he might need a little help. Four-year-olds were nothing if not persistent.

"It's like dogs," she told Maggie. "There are many different kinds of dogs. Some are big, some are small. But they're all still dogs. There are two different kinds of camels."

"Do the camels with one hump feel sad because they're different?"

Jeff leaned toward her. "Maybe the two-humped camels are the different ones."

Maggie's eyes unexpectedly filled with tears. "I don't want the camels to be sad."

Ashley hadn't seen that one coming. But before she could reach for her daughter and offer comfort, Jeff shocked her down to her toes by gently pulling the little girl onto his lap. He held her securely, as if he'd done it a thousand times before.

"Are you sad because you have brown hair?"

Maggie tilted her head so she could stare into his face. "No," she said slowly. "Mommy says I have pretty hair."

"Mommy's right. So you're not sad about how you look because you look perfect for you. Camels are the same. They know they're exactly what they should be.''

The tears disappeared as quickly as they'd arrived. "So camels are happy?"

"Nearly all the time."

Maggie beamed, then scrambled back to her seat where she picked up her spoon and went to work on her carrots. But Jeff didn't resume his own meal. Instead he continued to stare at the little girl.

"Maggie, you must promise me something. You must promise me to always be special and never change."

Maggie paused, her spoon half raised to her mouth. She grinned. "I'm gonna be a big girl soon."

"I know."

Something tightened in Ashley's chest. For the first time since she'd met Jeff Ritter, she knew what he was thinking. He was staring in wonder at her child and wishing life could always be exceptional for her. He wanted to protect her from all the bruises and scrapes she would encounter, both physical and emotional. Somehow little Maggie had found her way past Jeff's protective wall.

How was she supposed to resist a man who adored her daughter? To use her daughter's language, she would be very sad to leave this man. He'd only been a part of their lives for a short time, but he'd made an impact. When she returned to her already-in-progress life, nothing was going to be the same.

"What are you thinking?" Jeff asked, switching his attention to her.

"That Brenda was right. You're an honorable man."

He stiffened. "I'm no one's idea of a hero. Don't make me one."

She knew that there were ghosts in his past, but they didn't matter to her. He was honorable in the ways that counted. He would never leave a woman or a child in a bind. He was dependable. He wouldn't run off with the rent money, or borrow from a loan shark and disappear, leaving his wife to face the consequences. He was nothing like Damian.

Before she could explain what she meant, Jeff rose from the table. She glanced at his still half-full plate.

"Aren't you hungry?" she asked. "It's been a long time since lunch."

"I have work."

He left the kitchen without saying anything else. Maggie stared after him.

"Is Uncle Jeff mad?"

"No, honey, he's just busy."

And conflicted. Ashley sensed the battle within him. She knew that they were the reason, but she didn't know why. Part of her wanted to go after him and talk, but a part of her wanted to run in the opposite direction. Jeff might be logistically dependable, but he was still risky in other ways. She was determined to only get involved with a man who could love her unconditionally. Jeff wasn't in a place to love anyone. Not until he'd dealt with his past. Attraction was acceptable—which was good because she couldn't control hers. But anything else was foolhardy. And she'd already been a fool for a man more than once in her life. She wasn't about to do it again.

"Kirkman is worried about a kidnapping attempt," Zane said the following week when he and Jeff met to discuss their upcoming job in the Mediterranean.

Jeff studied the diagrams spread out on the large conference table. "Kidnapping's the least of it," he replied. "At least then there's the chance he'll be held for ransom. They'd want to keep him alive. If I were him, I'd be more concerned about an outright hit."

Zane grinned. "You want to tell him that?"

"Not especially." Jeff leaned back in his chair and glanced at his partner. "But I will when I meet with him next week."

"Rather you than me. I suspect he's something of a screamer."

"Screamer" was the indelicate term used to identify clients who couldn't handle the reality of their situation. They didn't want to hear about the actual or potential danger, and they frequently resisted making changes in their lifestyle to keep themselves and their family safe. Yet they were the first to start screaming the second something went wrong, most often when it was their own fault.

"I don't doubt it." But screamer or not, Kirkman had to be dealt with.

Zane tossed his pen onto the table and looked at his partner. "So, tell me about the woman in your life."

"There is no woman."

"That's not what the rumors say. And I happen to know that you have a female living in your house with you."

"She works for me. She's my new housekeeper."

Zane raised his dark eyebrows. "And?"

"And nothing. Her name is Ashley. She used to

work here in the office and now she works at my house. It's a business arrangement, nothing more.''

Even if he wanted it to be more, he wasn't going to act on the wanting. Because it would be dangerous for them both. He couldn't be what Ashley needed him to be, while she...

He returned his attention to the diagrams in front of him, even though he wasn't seeing anything remotely resembling the floor plan of the main villa. Instead he saw hazel eyes bright with laughter and inhaled a sweet scent he would remember for the rest of his life.

Ashley could be very important to him, he acknowledged. But he wasn't going to let that happen.

''What about her daughter?'' Zane asked. ''Kids can be tough to ignore.''

Jeff smiled. ''What would you know about children?''

''I know enough to avoid them,'' his partner joked. ''And so have you, until recently. So what's going on, Jeff? If you keep this up, people are going to start thinking you're actually human.''

It was an old joke—one that Jeff didn't find especially humorous. He also wasn't willing to answer any questions about Maggie. Not when the little girl was rapidly becoming important to him. Something had happened during the field trip to the zoo. Being with the children, taking care of Tommy when he'd skinned his hand, had cracked some part of his protection. Now Maggie slipped inside until he found himself thinking about her throughout the day, worrying about her. Would the teachers at the preschool remember to make sure she wore her jacket outside when she played? Did she finish her lunch? Had anyone treated her unfairly?

He still remembered when he'd actually taken her onto his lap to comfort her. His reaction had been pure instinct—and filled with more feelings than he cared to admit.

Both the Churchill females were making a mess of his life.

He pointed to the papers on the table. "We need the security plans finalized by the end of the week."

"No problem."

Zane leaned forward, resting his elbows on the table. Like Jeff, he wore a suit and tie to the office. Unlike Jeff, he tended to relax during the day, rolling up his sleeves and loosening his collar. He tapped the pages in front of them.

"I can do this myself," his partner said quietly. "It's time to let me take charge. You know, leave it to the younger guys."

"Why?" Jeff knew he wasn't getting old or soft. What was Zane's point?

"I can do this," Zane insisted.

"That was never a question."

"Wasn't it? Then why do you take all the dangerous assignments for yourself? You leave me baby-sitting the wives, while you stake out the trouble spots."

Jeff studied his partner. The man was only three or four years younger, but sometimes the age difference felt like decades. Zane had a lot of the same experiences, but he was a sharpshooter and a tactician. He'd spent most of his military years planning the operations or taking out the enemy from a distant location.

Zane had had his share of kills, but less experience with the horror.

"I don't have family," Jeff said. "The guy who has nothing to lose volunteers for the most dangerous job. It's an old habit. One I've had trouble breaking."

Zane's dark eyes never wavered. "Like I have a family to go home to?"

Jeff shrugged. Zane didn't have anyone in the world, either. "So we're even."

Zane frowned. "I thought—" He hesitated. "Hasn't that changed? I mean with the woman and the kid."

"Nothing's different."

Jeff's voice and words were firm. It was true, he told himself. Absolutely true. Having Ashley and Maggie in his life didn't change anything. He ignored the whispering voice deep inside that reminded him he was lying. Nothing had changed, he insisted to himself. He couldn't afford to let circumstances be different. He had to remember what had happened with Nicole—and the dream. Always the dream.

"I'd like the chance," Zane told him. "You owe me that."

Jeff looked at him. "Free license to kill yourself?"

"Isn't that what this job is about? Putting it all on the line for the client?"

Jeff knew that was true, but what he couldn't explain was why it made sense for him to do it over and over again, but when Zane wanted the same, Jeff couldn't help thinking it was a waste.

"I was at the bookstore at lunch," Jeff said, standing in the entrance of the kitchen and shifting his weight from foot to foot.

Ashley stopped stirring the pot of spaghetti sauce. Her boss actually looked nervous. He wouldn't meet her gaze and there was a distinct hint of color tingeing his cheeks. The mighty hunter embarrassed about something? She moved toward him, both intrigued and charmed.

"I had long suspected you could read," she told him. "But thanks for the confirmation."

His mouth twisted. "That's not the point. I have a trip coming up in a few weeks. I wanted a book for the flight home."

She started to ask about the flight there, then realized he would probably spend that preparing for whatever assignment he might be involved with.

"Okay," she said. "Well, I hope you enjoy your book and thanks for sharing the information with me."

"You're mocking me."

She couldn't help smiling. "Maybe just a little. Why are you telling me this?"

"Because there was a display of kids' books and I bought one for Maggie."

He moved his left arm. As he did so she realized that he'd had his left hand tucked behind his back. He held up a pink-and-white gift bag overflowing with glittering pink-gold tissue paper. Obviously he'd not only bought the book, but he'd had it wrapped, as well.

"Is it okay?" he asked.

She knew he wasn't asking about the presentation, but instead about the gift itself. Which left her with her own questions. Did he want to know if it was okay to give Maggie a book, or okay for him to give her daughter a present at all? Maybe he didn't know which he was asking, either.

Her chest tightened slightly as she remembered what had happened the previous week when Maggie had been upset about camels and Jeff had comforted her. He'd reacted impulsively. She'd seen the shock in his expression when he'd realized what he'd done, but by then it was too late to stop. Maggie was settled on his lap, leaning against him. Trusting and small, she was impossible to resist. Ashley knew—she'd been unable to keep from loving her from the moment she'd first held her.

But she was *supposed* to love her child. She'd wanted to have a baby and had been excited when her daughter had been born. But what about Jeff? Did he want children? He'd told her he couldn't have them. He'd also said that Maggie wasn't a substitute for his own child, but she was growing less confident of that. Did the little girl fill a hole in his heart Jeff didn't even know was there?

Ashley wasn't sure how she felt about her boss connecting with her child. She liked knowing he had a soft spot, but was she creating a problem for all of them?

He stepped forward and set the book on the table. ''You could tell her it was from you if that makes you more comfortable,'' he offered.

She shook her head. ''You give it to her,'' she said, even as she wondered why Maggie's father couldn't have been half as open to her presence in his life.

Damian had never had any interest in his child. He'd seen her as one more drain on his resources.

Jeff picked up the bag and headed for the family room. Faint sounds of an afternoon cartoon drifted through the house. Ashley followed him, wanting to see what happened yet knowing she was putting herself in danger by doing so.

"Uncle Jeff!" Maggie bounced to her feet when she saw him enter the room. She pushed the mute button on the television and grinned. "Whatcha got?"

"A present."

Big blue eyes widened. "For me?"

"Maybe."

Maggie grinned. "It's for me. What is it?"

"Why don't you find out for yourself?"

He held out the gift bag. The little girl practically vibrated with excitement. She took the offering and reverently placed it on the coffee table. Carefully she pulled out the tissue paper, then reached inside for the book.

Only, it wasn't just a book. An oddly shaped box held a storybook and a stuffed pink kitten. Maggie's mouth worked, but she couldn't make any sound. Obviously Jeff had figured out that anything feline was her favorite.

"Please read to me," she said, thrusting the box at him.

He freed both the book and the cat, handing the latter to her, then settled on the sofa. Maggie plopped down next to him, her body leaning against his, her expression joyful and trusting. She cradled her new stuffed cat in her arms.

Jeff opened the book. "'Once there was a pink

kitten named Pooky Girl, which was a rather silly name.'''

Maggie tugged on his suit sleeve. "This is the bestest present ever," she said.

"I'm glad you like it."

Ashley turned away. It wasn't that she didn't want to hear about the adventures of Pooky Girl, it was that she didn't want either Jeff or Maggie to notice the tears in her eyes.

Why did he have to be so darn *nice?* He was making her like him more than she should. He was making her think of him as warm and caring. That, combined with how hot he looked in jeans or in a suit, not to mention the tango her hormones performed every time he was within spitting distance, was enough to make her crazy. And dangerously vulnerable.

Jeff couldn't be a part of her life. He was too different. He was scary, although even as she said the words, she didn't believe them. Not anymore. But while she might have changed her opinion about him, one thing had stayed exactly the same. He was dangerous to her plans for the future. She wanted love and she had a bad feeling that Jeff's heart had died a long time ago.

It was well after midnight when Ashley awakened. She couldn't say what had startled her from sleep. The house was silent, and when she got up to check on her daughter, Maggie was sleeping peacefully in her bed and holding her new stuffed cat in her arms.

Ashley told herself it had been nothing and that she

should just go back to bed, but something compelled her to pick up her robe and head for the stairs.

"Oh, right. Like I'm going to check all the windows and doors," she muttered softly to herself as she walked onto the main floor.

Jeff's house was a fortress. She didn't understand his complex security system, and she knew that everything was safe. Even so she had to see for herself.

She checked the kitchen and Jeff's study, then headed to the front of the house. As she crossed by the living room, she saw a shadow by the window. Her mind froze, but her heart recognized. The nanosecond of fear faded.

Jeff.

He was looking out into the darkness, studying the night, or perhaps staring into a past that she couldn't begin to imagine.

He wore jeans and nothing else. His back was broad, his skin smooth. Muscles rippled and bunched as he shifted slightly. She felt her mouth water, something that had never occurred while she'd been looking at a man. Chocolate, sure. There was nothing like the smell of the confection to get her salivary glands all excited, but she hadn't noticed the same man-generated effect until this moment.

She had the strongest impulse to cross the room and touch him. To stroke his bare skin, to press her mouth to his shoulder and taste him. A shiver rippled through her. It was just hormones, she told herself. She was in the middle of her cycle, so biologically she was predisposed to want sex. Mother Nature at work. But her desire didn't *mean* anything—not in the real sense of the word. It was interesting information she wasn't about to act on.

"I'm sorry I woke you."

Jeff's voice cut through the night, startling her. She hadn't realized he knew she was there. "No. You didn't. I just..." She couldn't explain how she'd come to be awake. "Sometimes I'm compelled to cruise through the house, making sure things are the way they should be. What's your excuse for being awake at this indecent hour?"

She'd made the comment lightly, but when he didn't instantly answer, she realized she might have crossed over some invisible line in their relationship.

"Sorry," she said quickly. "I was making conversation, not prying. You don't have to answer that."

"I don't mind." His voice was low and hoarse— as if speaking were difficult for him. "I have a recurring dream. It wakes me up and it's a while before I can get back to sleep."

She suspected his dreams weren't anything like hers in which she found out she had a final exam in a class she'd never attended or was supposed to pick up her daughter but suddenly couldn't remember the address of the preschool.

"Want to talk about it? Sometimes that helps."

She made the offer without thinking, then thought about retracting it. After all, did she really want to know the deep dark secrets trapped in Jeff's subconscious?

He shoved his hands into his jeans pockets. He still stood with his back to her. "I—" He cleared his throat. "There's a village. It's on fire. As I walk through it, I realize the people there are more frightened of me than of the destruction of the flames.''

Ashley listened to the stark words as he told her what happened. She took a step toward him, visualizing the running children, hearing their cries of pain and fear. Her breath caught when he told her what he saw in the reflection of the shallow pool.

Not human? Is that what he really thought?

''No, Jeff,'' she said, moving closer still. ''I'll admit that you're a little intimidating, and until I got to know you I thought you were a little scary, but I never saw you as other than a man. And Maggie's adored you from the beginning.''

''She's very special.''

''So are you,'' she told him. ''You're not the easiest guy to get to know, but you have many wonderful qualities.''

He glanced at her over his shoulder. ''My ex-wife, Nicole, wouldn't agree.''

''Then she's wrong.''

He still faced the window. The room was too dark for her to see his reflection clearly, but she could see the shadow. He shook his head.

''Nicole saw the truth,'' he said slowly. ''She knew what I was. She said she was glad we never had children together. She told me that the reason I couldn't have a baby wasn't because of my low sperm count but because I wasn't human anymore. I'd become a soldier and in the process, I'd forgotten how to be just a man.''

''No,'' Ashley breathed, as she instinctively reached out and rested her fingers on his bare shoul-

der. "No, that's not true at all. You're just as human
as the rest of us. Just as—"

Without warning, he spun to face her and grabbed
her hand. His touch was strong and firm, but not
bruising.

"Don't touch me," he growled. "Don't start something you can't finish."

For a second she thought she'd violated some
fighter code. That touching him made him think he
was being threatened and put her in danger. But then
she noticed that he hadn't released her fingers and was
instead rubbing them with his own. There was something sensual about the caress. Something that made
her bones start to melt.

"Jeff?"

He stared at her and she wondered how she could
have ever thought of his eyes as cold. They weren't
cold at all. Instead fire raged in them. Fire and need
and a hunger that made her lick her lips in anticipation.

She might not have a whole lot of experience with
men, but she recognized the powerful desire ripping
through him. He was a barely controlled, sexually
ready male.

She should have turned and run for the hills. Or at
the very least, her own bedroom. Wasn't there a lock
on the door? Wouldn't she be safe there?

Except she found she didn't want to be safe. Not
when the alternative was being held in Jeff's arms.
She felt her own body flaring to life. Needs long de-
nied awoke and stretched, making her ache.

Slowly, very slowly so he could know what she
was about to do, she reached toward him with her

free hand and placed her fingers on his chest. She felt warm skin, cool, crinkly hair and a faint tremor.

He swore and clutched her shoulders. "Ashley."

The way he said her name made her want to purr. There was desperation in his voice, and a hunger that cried out from the soul. She raised herself on her toes and pressed her lips to his.

"I have every intention of finishing this," she murmured against his mouth. "So what are you waiting for?"

Chapter Nine

Ashley should have known that she would be in no way prepared for his kiss. Jeff's strong arms came around her and he pulled her against him. She'd barely absorbed the feel of his rock-hard body, so unyielding against her own, when his lips claimed hers in a moment of possessive need that robbed her of all will.

He didn't explore or ask or hesitate. Instead he pressed his mouth against hers as if his life depended on them kissing at that exact moment. His aggression should have frightened her, she thought hazily, except she felt that she needed him just as much. There wasn't any air in her lungs and he was her only source of life.

She parted for him instantly, not needing to be seduced, but instead wanting to be taken. She wanted to experience possession at Jeff's hands.

He was a man. She'd been with men before—she had the child to prove it. But no other man had kissed her in quite the same way. Maybe it was a soldier's attention to detail; maybe it was just good luck on her part. Because instead of accepting her silent invitation to invade her mouth, he continued to kiss her lips. He was aggressive and demanding, yet his barely suppressed violence left her feeling feminine and tender. He slowly explored her lips, making her shiver with anticipation.

Mouth on mouth, hands on body. Their breath became one. Finally, when he'd discovered her to his satisfaction, he finally stroked her bottom lip with his tongue. The damp heat made her knees tremble. She clutched at his shoulders, needing to anchor herself in a suddenly spinning universe.

Finally, when she was sure she couldn't take it anymore, he slipped into her mouth.

She gasped. If she'd had the breath or strength, she would have screamed. At the first stroke of his tongue against hers, fire ripped through her body. Her breasts swelled, and between her legs a sensation of heaviness and desire made her squirm.

He tasted completely masculine and perfectly of himself. He stroked her, teased her, discovered her. He was completely in control and she found that made her relax. There was no reason to worry about being awkward. Jeff wouldn't let her misstep. Lack of fear allowed anticipation to build. She raised herself on tiptoe so she could fit herself more fully to him, absorbing his strength. His large hands began to stroke up and down her back.

She arched into his touch. She wore a cotton nightgown and a flannel robe. Underneath both garments was a cotton pair of panties. Suddenly the layers were heavy and unnecessary. She wanted to feel his fingers against her bare skin. She wanted the same attention to detail that he gave to their kiss brought to her breasts and other parts of her body.

He cupped her face and held her slightly away from him. His gray eyes burned bright with need. His fingers trembled slightly, and she was aware of the hard ridge of his desire pressing against her belly.

"Ashley, I—" His voice was low and hoarse, as if it was difficult for him to speak. "I need you to be sure."

She managed a shaky smile. "I'm very sure," she whispered. "I know it's crazy for about a thousand reasons, but I want you."

She blushed as she spoke, not used to being so bold. But she didn't call the words back. She did want Jeff more than she'd ever wanted anyone. Even the man she'd been married to.

He ran his fingers through her mussed hair, then dropped a quick kiss to her mouth. "I don't have any protection with me." He shrugged. "I don't sleep around much, I've had a recent blood test and I'm not exactly a pregnancy risk."

She couldn't help smiling. How like Jeff to reassure her that she was safe with him.

She leaned forward and pressed her mouth against his bare chest. He tasted faintly of salt. "Did you think I would want to stop?"

He didn't answer with words. Instead he pressed his mouth to hers and hauled her up against him. They kissed deeply and she felt herself disappearing into the experience. Perhaps later she would think that she was crazy for giving in. Perhaps after they'd crossed the line that would change everything, she would have regrets, but not now. Not this night. She sensed that as much as Jeff wanted her, he needed her even more. And it was that need that made him impossible to deny. Well, that and her own aching body that longed for the release *his* body promised.

He moved his head slightly so that he could kiss her cheek, then her jaw. Damp kisses tickled her skin and made her gasp. He moved lower, down her neck to the collar of her robe. Once there, he exchanged lips for hands and continued his journey. She sucked in a breath as his hands found and cupped her breasts. Before she could beg him to never, ever stop, he slipped to her waist and her hips. His thumbs brushed the jutting bones there.

Ashley had a moment of feeling self-conscious. She knew that she was too skinny by at least ten or fifteen pounds. At one time she'd been a tad more lush, but a limited food budget, not to mention the need to provide for her child, had changed that. Still, Jeff didn't seem to be complaining.

Instead he dropped to his knees. Once there he pushed at her robe and nightgown, shoving them up to her waist, then moving her hands so that she would hold the fabric. He tugged on her panties, pulling them down. Without thinking, she stepped out of them.

Ashley felt heat climbing her face. He couldn't possibly be going to— It was too soon and he was... Well, he just couldn't.

But he could and he did. Before she'd figured out

a way to act casual about the whole thing, he pressed his mouth to her belly. The kiss touched her down to her soul and made her gasp his name.

He tenderly nibbled along the sensitive skin there, pausing only to tease her belly button. Her legs began to tremble. She had to brace herself to keep upright. He moved lower and lower still until he reached the most secret part of her. Once there, he gently parted the protective folds of her feminine place and licked her.

Ashley bit her lip to keep from screaming. Inside her head, a thousand voices echoed with a single cry of pleasure. It was as if he knew her better than she knew herself, she thought hazily, barely able to remain upright as he kissed her over and over.

He urged her to shift so she could part her legs. She tried to do as he requested, but it was too difficult to maintain her balance. Suddenly she stumbled and was falling, only to be caught in his strong embrace.

Jeff smiled at her as he lowered her to the carpet in the living room. He settled her on her rear, then carefully drew her robe off her shoulders and pulled her nightgown over her head. She was naked and found that she didn't much mind. It felt right with him. Maybe a sensible woman would have been nervous or even scared, but all she could think was that she wanted him to pick up exactly where he'd left off.

Unfortunately he didn't read her mind. However, what he did instead turned out to be just as wonderful. He bent over her breast and drew one tight nipple into his mouth. The other received attention from his fingers. He licked, he nibbled, he teased until she was writhing on the floor and desperate for more.

After he'd switched so that her other breast had equal attention, he shifted so that he knelt between her legs and kissed his way down her stomach. Her breath caught as she stiffened in anticipation. Finally he bent low to give her the most intimate kiss of all. The one that made her cry out his name as she drew back her knees and dug her heels into the carpet.

His hands cupped her hips. His breath was hot, his tongue insistent. She couldn't stand what he was doing to her. Not for another second.

"Don't stop," she gasped. "Please."

She felt more than heard a low, throaty sound of laughter as he continued his ministrations. Then suddenly the world tilted and flew out of control. Before she could prepare herself, a powerful wave of release crashed through her. She was caught up and carried away, drowning in the most amazing sensations she'd ever experienced.

Once again Jeff caught her in his strong arms. Caught her and held her as she slowly, very slowly, returned to normal.

When she finally surfaced enough to open her eyes, she found herself staring into his face. He smiled down at her. She felt her own lips curve in response.

"Mission accomplished," she murmured. "They teach you that at boot camp?"

"No. In special forces. I took the advanced course."

Her own smile turned into a grin. "Jeff, you could teach the course."

He touched her face, then smoothed back her hair.

"I wanted it to be good for you," he told her. "I'm glad you were pleased."

"*Pleased* doesn't begin to describe it."

He was so gentle, she thought. Despite the fire still raging inside of him. She felt the insistent pressure of his arousal. He was as hungry as she had been just a few moments before. Yet he'd taken the time to satisfy her very thoroughly. This from a man who dreamed he wasn't human and kept mostly to himself?

She wanted to ask what it meant that they were doing this. But even more, she wanted to feel his bare skin against hers as he entered her.

She stroked his back, then slid her hands around to his chest. "I think it's time for the second act," she said and brought his mouth to hers.

As they kissed, he moved his fingers against her breasts, then slipped them lower. She was still slick and swollen and it didn't take much to get her blood boiling all through her. In a matter of minutes she was writhing against him, as hungry as she'd been before.

He shifted so that he could pull off his jeans, then returned to kneel between her legs. The only light in the room came from outside—a diffused illumination from the streetlights' glow in the damp night. His face was in shadows and she couldn't see his eyes. Yet she wasn't afraid. Not even when she felt his arousal pressing against her.

She slipped a hand between them to guide him inside. With one smooth thrust, he filled her completely. She gasped as her muscles relaxed to admit him, then immediately tightened around his width.

He braced himself on his hands and stared into her eyes. She kept her gaze on him. Even as he entered her again and again, even as her own body began to react to the tension filling her, she refused to look away.

Jeff knew he wasn't going to be able to last much longer. His lack of control wasn't about not having been with a woman in a long time, although that was true enough. Instead his legendary self-control was being destroyed by a wide-eyed gaze and the feel of slick walls contracting in pleasure.

He felt the first release ripple through Ashley's slender body. She clutched his arms and arched back her head, all the while gasping for breath and pleading with him to follow. He told himself to hold back. That his waiting would make it better for her. But suddenly he didn't have a choice. He couldn't wait, couldn't do anything but fill her again and again, shifting back on his haunches as he grabbed her hips and pulled her closer.

And then he was at the point of no return. He thrust into her deeply, making them both cry out. He surrendered to the release, losing himself in a perfect moment of paradise.

Jeff rolled over and pulled Ashley into his arms. The night was still except for the sound of their breathing. She cuddled against him, her head on his shoulder, her breath tickling his chest.

''When was the last time you did it on your living room floor?'' she asked.

''Never.''

He thought about telling her more. That he'd never

invited a woman to his house. He'd never made love here before.

Made love.

The words stopped him, but he couldn't deny them. Ashley was more than just sex.

"What about you?" he asked.

She propped herself up on her elbow and grinned down at him. "I've never made love on your living room floor before, either."

Her humor made him wrap his arms around her and pull her against him. He liked the feel of her naked body pressing into his.

"How do you feel?" he asked as he stroked her from shoulders to rear.

"Good. Better than good." She sighed. "You were pretty amazing. All that ability to focus on the task at hand. I should have guessed how well it would translate. Now if only my rug burn will fade by morning."

"Rug burn?"

He started to sit up to look at her back, but she laughed and pushed him back onto the carpet.

"I'm kidding. My back is completely unscathed."

"Good."

She turned onto her side. He slid his hands over her hip and felt the prominent bone. "You're too thin," he told her.

She glared. "I take back all those nice things I just said. It's incredibly tacky to criticize a woman's body at any time, but never more so than after you'd just done the wild thing and while she's still naked."

She was being playful, but he didn't smile. "I'm not being critical, I'm stating a fact. You haven't been eating enough. Why do I know that it's more about money than looking good in clothes?''

She sat up and turned so she was facing away from him. ''Don't, Jeff. I don't want to talk about that. Please don't spoil the mood.''

Her request answered his question. He hated that money had been so tight for her that there were times when she didn't get enough to eat. He wanted to fix her life. He needed to make it better. Except he was the wrong person for the job. Nicole had been right when she'd pointed out that he didn't know how to be like other men. At least he'd given Ashley a good job. As long as she worked for him, she would be safe.

''You're supposed to say something reassuring,'' she muttered.

''I'm sorry.'' He touched her bare skin. ''I don't want to spoil the mood. Please come back here and let me hold you.''

She turned toward him. The lamplight filtered through the partially open drapes, illuminating her body. Her breasts were surprisingly full for her slight frame. The nipples were tight. As she moved, her breasts swayed slightly. She was an erotic image brought to life by the night.

Unable to stop himself, he leaned over and took her right nipple in his mouth. She grasped his head and moaned. Suddenly he was touching her everywhere, needing her, desperate for her. He told himself that it was too soon.

''I don't want to hurt you,'' he murmured.

''Don't worry about it.''

She pressed herself against him as they kissed.

He was hard in a heartbeat. Hard and hungry, as if they hadn't made love less than an hour before. He cupped her breasts and teased her nipples. She ran her fingers through his hair and down his back. He put his hands on her hips and urged her to straddle him. She did so; then in one easy, sexy movement she settled on top of him and let him find his way home.

Ashley couldn't believe they were making love again. She was generally a once-every-three-or-four-days kind of girl. But with Jeff she couldn't seem to get enough. The second he began to fill her, she felt herself contracting around him. The first release made her arch her head back in an attempt to catch her breath. The second made her frantic to have him fill her more and more and more.

She raised and lowered herself with a pace she thought might be too fast until she realized that his hands guided her hips, keeping her in place and her rhythm steady for both of them. Every few seconds another contraction filled her. She hadn't known it could be like this.

Suddenly tension spiraled through her. Tension and need. It consumed her until she had no choice but to shudder with the glory of it all. Just as she reached her pinnacle, she felt Jeff stiffen and cry out. Together they clung to each other as their bodies reveled in the moment of being one.

Ashley slept like one of the innocent, Jeff thought later when they were both in his large bed. Her even breathing spoke of her rest. He couldn't find the same solace; he didn't dare.

When was the last time he'd made love? Not had

sex, but actually made love with a woman? He couldn't recall. Not since Nicole. And with her it had been before things had started to go so desperately wrong. Sex was a bodily function. He understood and respected his body's need for release. But this was different.

He closed his eyes but didn't allow himself to sleep because the dream lurked in the world of the unconscious and he didn't want to have it twice in one night. Not with Ashley sleeping so peacefully beside him. She might think that she understood him, but she had no idea of his real self.

So instead of sleeping he held her close, ignoring the very male part of him that wanted her again. He told himself that the wanting was allowed for this night but no longer, because wanting was dangerous. Wanting made a man weak and careless. Either could get him killed.

In the morning he would walk away without looking back. He would never allow himself to do this again or even to think of it. That would be best for both of them. But until morning there was the night. He closed his eyes and breathed in the sweet scent of her skin.

The next morning Ashley was fighting both a mild case of rug burn and a major case of the guilts. She tried to act as normal as possible as she fixed her daughter's lunch, even though Jeff was also sitting at the table, looking as if nothing had happened the previous night. Fortunately Maggie didn't sense the tension between the adults and chattered away as if this was an ordinary morning.

Ashley had awakened to the sound of Jeff in the shower and had used the moment of privacy to escape to her own room. When they'd met up in the kitchen, she'd managed to greet him and pour him coffee without melting into a puddle of desire, or worse, clueing in her daughter that something was different.

As she spread peanut butter on bread, Ashley tried to reconcile the well-dressed conservative man sitting at the table with the one who had licked her entire body the night before. Or the one who had awakened her just before dawn so they could make love yet again. She couldn't wait for round two.

Just hold on one minute, she told herself as she reached for the jar of jelly. There wasn't going to be a round two. Last night had been amazing. It had been special and perfect and it had to be a one-time event. Jeff wasn't the kind of man a woman like her settled down with, and she didn't want a casual, sexual relationship. For her, the act of physical intimacy had always been closely tied to love. She didn't love Jeff; she didn't want to love Jeff. To make sure that didn't change, she was going to have to stay out of his bed.

She would tell him as soon as they were alone.

That decided, she finished her daughter's sandwich and put it in the small, plastic, cat-covered lunch box.

"It's gonna be Easter soon," Maggie was saying.

Jeff smiled at the little girl over his coffee mug. "What happens then?"

Maggie looked shocked that he didn't know. "Mommy and me go to church where they have lots and lots of pretty flowers and we listen to the min—min—" She glanced at her mother for help.

"The minister," Ashley said.

Maggie beamed. "And when we come home we find what the Easter bunny left for me. Last year he was very nice and left me lots of chocolate." She leaned toward Jeff and lowered her voice. "I'm hopin' he's nice to me this year."

Maggie turned to her mother. "Mommy, can I take my new book to school to show my teacher?"

Ashley nodded.

Maggie jumped from her seat and raced toward the stairs. Which, unfortunately, left Ashley alone with Jeff. He turned his attention to her.

"How are you feeling?"

Was it her imagination or did his tone sound different this morning? She barely stopped from slapping herself in the forehead. Of course it was different. *They* were different. Their intimacy the previous night had changed everything.

"I, ah, I'm fine," she said, barely able to meet his gaze.

She could feel the heat flaring on her cheeks. What was he thinking? Was he, too, remembering what it had been like when they'd been together? Should she tell him now that it had been wonderful but really couldn't happen again?

"Jeff, I—"

"I found it! I found it!" Maggie's singsong voice filled the kitchen as the little girl flew into the room, her new book clutched to her chest.

She dashed over to Jeff and flung herself into his arms. "Thank you for my book. And the kitty. They're my bestest presents ever."

Ashley watched her daughter's small arms go trustingly around Jeff's neck. She saw the large man she now knew to be tender and considerate, hug her back. Suddenly she was aware of the sound of her own heartbeat and the way the room seemed to tilt slightly.

She'd been worried about getting involved with a man who wasn't right for her. She'd been concerned about having her heart engaged in futile longing for a man who could never love her back. But she'd never once thought anyone else was at risk.

Now, as she observed the tall, dangerous man and the trusting little girl, she knew that Maggie was the one who had already given her heart away. Maggie had bonded with Jeff, viewing him as the father she never had. Maggie would have dreams and expectations, and there was nothing Ashley could do to warn her about holding back.

An ache filled Ashley's chest. She wanted to protect her daughter, but she didn't know how. Should they leave? Should they—

Jeff whispered something in Maggie's ear and her daughter laughed. Ashley knew it was too late to keep Maggie from connecting with Jeff. And taking her away now, before they had to go, seemed cruel. Perhaps it would be best to let the child enjoy Jeff while they were in his house. Later they would both have to deal with the impossible task of getting over Jeff Ritter.

Chapter Ten

Jeff left his office with the Kirkman file under his arm. He knew he could have asked Brenda to do the research on the small town just neighboring the Mediterranean estate, but he needed something with which to distract himself. Something that would take his mind off Ashley.

They hadn't spoken that morning. Maggie provided a perfect buffer and he hadn't seen the point of trying to get Ashley alone for a few minutes of conversation. It was ironic. He who had faced numerous terrorists, enemy soldiers and certain-death assignments without flinching was nervous about talking with a woman. He grimaced. Nervous didn't begin to describe how he felt. He was flat-out terrified.

He didn't know why she'd agreed to make love with him last night. He'd told her about the dream;

he'd bared something close to the truth about who and what he was. And yet she hadn't run away. Maybe she hadn't figured out what it all meant. Maybe that would come later.

He didn't want to think about that. He didn't want to see her features tighten in disgust or fear. He didn't want her backing away from him when he entered a room.

And yet, despite all that could still go wrong, he wasn't sorry. How could he be? Last night had been perfect.

He stepped into the research room and settled at one of the specially programmed computers. Even as he typed on the keyboard, he thought about what it had been like to be with her. How she'd looked and felt and tasted. How she'd sounded. The way that she'd clung to him, losing herself in the moment.

No, he couldn't be sorry about that. Even if it meant that he could never sleep again.

He frowned slightly. The dreams lurked in the back of his mind, an ever-present enemy. He knew that they would extract their revenge for his temporary assumption that he could be like everyone else.

"Where's Brenda?"

The question came from behind him. Jeff turned and saw his partner lounging in the doorway to the research room. Zane raised a questioning eyebrow and continued, "Did she call in sick?"

"No. She's around."

Zane sauntered over to the chair next to Jeff's and took a seat. "So why are you in here?"

Jeff shrugged. "I had the time."

Zane didn't look convinced. "Are you all right?

You haven't been yourself for the past few days and today it's worse.''

"What are you talking about? What's worse?"

"I'm not sure." Zane studied him. "It's the woman, isn't it? The one staying at your house."

Jeff didn't think he'd been acting any differently, but obviously he'd been wrong. Zane was observant and he didn't make mistakes.

"Nothing's changed," he bluffed, knowing it was a lie. Having Ashley and Maggie come live with him was just the first of many changes.

"Don't get me wrong," Zane told him. "I think you having a woman around is a good thing. I'm all in favor of that. You need some normalcy."

Jeff didn't agree, but he wasn't about to argue. Ashley was dangerous to him because she distracted him. In his line of work, a distraction could cause a mistake. Just one misstep, one unnoticed detail, would mean the difference between living and dying.

Zane jerked his head toward the open door. "You ready for the meeting?"

Jeff glanced at his watch, then nodded. They had four new recruits going through orientation. A quiet, competent woman in her early thirties, and three ex-military men.

"What do you think?" he asked his partner as he closed his folder and followed Zane out of the research office.

"They're all right. The youngest of the three, Sanders, is a little gung ho for my liking. He still thinks the protection business is glamorous."

Jeff grimaced. "Just what we need. Someone stupid. How'd he get this far?"

"Great credentials and impeccable recommendations. They're genuine," Zane continued as he paused just outside the conference room. "I checked them myself."

Then they hadn't been faked, Jeff thought. Zane didn't make those kind of mistakes, either.

Jeff stepped into the conference room with Zane on his heels. Jack Delaney, former Secret Service agent and arms expert, nodded as his bosses walked to the front of the room. The four recruits sat at a conference table facing the podium. Jeff looked them over, noticing the even gazes that met his own. The woman sat a little apart from the rest. She had long red hair and a body that would make traffic stand still. He briefly wondered what had brought someone that good-looking to this line of work, then dismissed the question. Her appearance didn't matter if she was the best.

He glanced at the three men. The youngest was easy to pick out. He wore a grin the size of Texas.

"These are the men who sign your paychecks," Jack said easily. "Jeff Ritter and Zane Rankin." He nodded and stepped away from the podium.

Jeff took his place. He looked at each of the recruits, trying to size them up. Only two people would be hired and that decision wouldn't be made for at least a month. He and Zane were particular about whom they worked with. After all, the team members risked their lives together. To trust that much, everyone had to depend on each other.

"There is no room for mistakes," he said by way of introduction. "Nor do we bring our egos, our tempers or our prejudices to any assignment. Every job puts it all on the line. Before we invite you to join our company, we will attempt to find out your weaknesses, your faults and what makes your skin crawl. Because the kind of clients who employ us expect the best.''

He paused to make sure he had their attention. ''A British banker had handled some delicate foreign transactions a couple of years back. He noticed that there were some irregularities and traced them to the source. Along the way, he discovered his bank was being used to launder billions in drug money. The men responsible for the deposits were not pleased to be exposed. In an effort to keep the man quiet, they kidnapped his only child. The man's wife had died in childbirth. He had no other relatives.''

Jeff leaned forward, resting his elbows on the podium. ''A half-dozen kidnappers holding one small boy. There was no margin for error. As it turns out, we got lucky. A clean shot from a hundred yards. How many of you would be comfortable in those circumstances? No second chance, no room for errors.''

He didn't wait for anyone to answer. ''In case you're wondering why you didn't read about this in the paper, it's because that's how we prefer to work. While there is occasional press coverage, it's the exception rather than the rule. If you're in this for glamour, fame or a chance to get laid, tell me now.''

This time he did pause. The woman grinned. ''Gee, boss, and I was so in it for the sex.''

Her comment made everyone chuckle, easing the tension in the room.

''Kidding aside,'' Jeff said when the room was quiet again. ''Each of you has to question if you have what it takes. The best operatives are loners. No connections, no ties. It's harder to be afraid when you have nothing to lose. Good luck.''

With that he turned and walked out of the room. Zane would speak next, but Jeff had heard the speech a couple dozen times. Besides, he was too distracted by his own thoughts to pay attention.

He'd told the recruits the truth. It took having nothing to lose to stop being afraid. He'd lived by that code for years; it gave him his edge. But what if that had all changed? He hadn't been able to stop thinking about Ashley. She haunted him like a sensual ghost determined to win his soul. He couldn't afford the distraction. He couldn't afford to get involved.

If he felt pleasure, what would be next? Weakness? Hesitation? Would he worry about her to the point where he would hesitate a split second?

That wasn't an option. There was only one solution to the problem. He could never be intimate with her again.

Ashley knew she was grinning like a sheep but she couldn't help herself. There was something wonderful about the way her thighs hurt from what she'd been doing the previous night. Okay, yes, she knew that she and Jeff could never have a normal relationship. And yes, having an affair with one's boss, however brief, was never clever. But there was something to be said for a romantic, and slightly sexual, glow.

She felt as if she wasn't actually touching the ground when she walked. Everything seemed more brightly colored and nothing could upset her good mood. The downside was she'd had a darned difficult time concentrating in class. She'd found herself doodling Jeff's name instead of paying attention to the lecture.

She had it bad.

Ashley walked to the refrigerator to pull out the chicken she wanted to roast for dinner. As much as she wanted to be with Jeff again, she knew that it could never work between them. There was no future here. She wanted to make a safe haven for herself and her daughter. She had no clue as to what Jeff wanted, but she suspected it was something very different. He wasn't the kind of man who would love her more than anything. He would never promise to love her unconditionally, the way she would want to love him.

She froze in the act of removing the chicken from the shelf. Not that she was saying she loved Jeff. She didn't. She liked him a lot and she thought he was hot, which was very different from love. Jeff was not the man for her—he had a past that was too different from her own. They obviously couldn't make love again, even if he wanted to. She would have to tell him as soon as he got home.

Jeff couldn't remember another more cowardly act in his life. However potentially difficult or painful, he'd never taken the easy way out until tonight. Instead of coming home at his usual time and facing Ashley, he'd had Brenda phone to say he had to work late.

It was after eleven when he pulled into the garage and turned off the engine. The situation had been worse than he'd realized. Not only didn't he want to face her, he hadn't been able to stop thinking about her while he'd been at the office. Despite his long hours, he hadn't gotten anything accomplished.

He climbed out of the car and headed for the house. As he'd driven up, he'd noticed faint light from behind the drapes, so he wasn't surprised to see that Ashley had left on a few lamps. As he crossed toward the kitchen, he tried to remember if he'd ever not come home in the dark.

He found a piece of paper waiting for him on the kitchen table. "Uncle Jeff" spelled out in very uneven, very large block crayon letters was followed by an arrow pointing to a plate with a slice of chocolate cake. The dessert looked too tidy to have been made by Maggie, but the welcoming note was pure little girl.

His chest tightened. He couldn't recall anyone ever doing something like this for him. Maggie had actually thought about him while he'd been gone. Had Ashley, as well?

His house was no longer empty and impersonal. He told himself it didn't matter, but it did. He told himself he shouldn't like it—but he did.

Swearing under his breath, he ignored the dessert and headed for the stairs. He had to get himself under control. Distractions weren't allowed. He promised himself the situation would get better with time. It had to.

She was waiting in his bed. Jeff stepped into the room and flipped the switch. Ashley lay curled up on top of the covers, one arm bent and supporting her head. She wore a lace nightgown that covered everything and concealed nothing. He forgot to breathe.

"Hi," she said, slowly pushing herself into a sitting position. "I wasn't sure what time you'd be home and I didn't want to miss you."

He couldn't speak. He could barely set down his briefcase. His throat was tight, his groin was on fire. He didn't care. He wanted to spend the rest of his life looking at her slender curves and remembering what it had been like to make love with her.

"It's about Easter," she said. She sounded calm. She *looked* calm.

He blinked. He couldn't have heard her correctly. "Easter?"

"You know, that holiday we have in the spring? Maggie's been talking about it, as you may remember. The thing is, I always hide Easter eggs for her. I would like to know if it's all right for me to do that in your yard this year." She wrinkled her nose. "Unless it rains. That would be a drag."

He couldn't understand what she was saying. Didn't she know she was practically naked and making him crazy, lying there on his mattress? Yet she acted as if everything were perfectly fine.

"Use the yard," he managed to say. "For the eggs."

"Good. Also, when I talked to Brenda today, she invited us to brunch at her house. I hope you don't mind that I said yes. So I figured we'd do the Easter egg hunt, then go to church, then over to Brenda's. Of course if you object to church, you could meet us there."

He was losing his mind. "Brenda invited the three of us?"

Some of her calmness faded. He sensed her tension. Suddenly Ashley wouldn't look at him. "Yes, well,

I thought that was odd. Then I figured she'd run it past you and you'd agreed.''

Brenda hadn't said a word.

Ashley slid to the edge of the bed, then stood. She was barefoot and nearly naked.

''The thing is, I'd told myself I was going to be practical,'' she said, moving closer to him. Her hazel eyes glinted with humor. ''Having an affair with my boss is not only crazy, it's potentially dangerous. I have goals, you have goals and they're not the same, right?''

He suddenly wanted to hear all about her goals. Instead he nodded.

''So it would be dumb to get involved.''

As she spoke, she put her hands on his shoulders and pushed off his jacket. The thick fabric slid down his arms and slipped to the ground.

She pressed her fingers against his chest. ''But you're so darned cute when you're all stoic and sol-dierlike. I'm not sure I can resist that. There's also the way you're patient with Maggie and incredible in bed. All that attention focused on what I want. Call me spineless. One minute I was getting ready to crawl between my own sheets and the next I was here. Want me to go away?''

Instead of answering with words, he cupped her face in his hands and kissed her. She responded the instant his mouth brushed hers, leaning into him and groaning softly. Desire filled him, making his blood heat and his arousal flex against her belly. He wanted her. He'd been fooling himself by thinking he could share the same house and ignore her.

He swept his tongue against her lower lip. She

parted for him, but he waited before entering, brushing back and forth until she trembled. Only then did he slip inside and taste her sweetness.

She clung to him. Bodies pressed, heat flared, need grew. He felt the rapid pounding of her heartbeat and knew that his own beat just as fast. Desperate for more, he broke the kiss so he could nibble his way along her jaw and down her throat. She groaned and arched her head back.

"Jeff," she gasped. "You don't have to do the Easter thing if you don't want to. I mean I won't change my mind about wanting to make love with you."

He couldn't help chuckling as he tugged on her lace nightgown. "I'll do the Easter thing," he said softly, pulling down her short sleeves and baring her to the waist. "Right now I'll promise to do anything you want."

Chapter Eleven

Jeff awakened shortly before dawn. He jerked out of a sound sleep only to find himself right where he was supposed to be—in his bedroom. It was nearly a full second before he was able to register two important facts: he hadn't had the dream and he wasn't alone.

He didn't know which startled him more. After he and Ashley had made love the previous evening, they'd slipped under the covers. He'd held her close, fully expecting to spend another night staring at the ceiling, not daring to close his eyes and experience the nightmare. Instead he'd drifted off without being haunted by the specters of his past.

He turned toward the feminine warmth pressing against him, only to find Ashley watching him. She smiled slowly.

"Good morning."

Her voice was velvet, her body silk. He found himself instantly aroused by her presence and the acceptance he saw in her eyes.

"How'd you sleep?" he asked, turning toward her and touching her cheek.

"Really well." She hesitated. "At the risk of starting your day with the words every man hates to hear...we have to talk."

Her hair was a mess. Dark curls teased at her face and shot out in every direction like an uneven halo. Her skin was slightly flushed and the scent of their lovemaking clung to the sheets. Her need to have a conversation didn't disturb what he considered a perfect moment.

He knew what she was going to say. A casual relationship with him wasn't her style. This wasn't sensible; they had to end it. He told himself that he didn't mind. The past two nights had been more than he'd expected. They would be enough.

"Talk away," he said easily, propping his head on one hand.

"Oh, sure. Make me be the one." She flopped onto her back, then turned her head toward him. "Jeff, what are we doing?"

He wanted to say they had been sleeping and now they were having a discussion, but he knew that wasn't exactly what she meant. "What would you like us to be doing?"

"If anyone else gave me that answer, I would instantly accuse the man of hedging, but I suspect you're asking because you genuinely want to know. Am I right?"

He nodded. She wanted to talk about *them*. About their potentially mutual goals and desires. He didn't have either—at least none that included a normal relationship with a very nice woman.

She pressed her lips together. "I'm going to take a wild guess here and say that I think you're out of your element with me. Am I right?"

He nodded again. Now it was his turn to settle onto his back.

"Jeff, is there anyone special in your life?"

He knew what she was asking. "No. I wouldn't be here with you if there was."

"That's what I thought but I had to be sure." She slid her hand toward him under the covers and lightly touched his arm. "Has there been anyone special recently?"

He thought about the question. Recently there had been no one. "No. There hasn't been anyone in my life since Nicole."

And in an odd way, Nicole hadn't been in his life at all. The young man she'd married had disappeared in a matter of months. By their second anniversary, it was as if that Jeffrey Ritter had never existed.

He saw now that he shouldn't have married her. Or having married her, he shouldn't have gone into Special Forces. He'd changed so much so quickly. Their marriage had never had a chance. As for other women since then, they had existed but not the way Ashley meant. They had been nameless, faceless companions of the night. Strangers who welcomed him for an hour or a day. One woman had hung on for nearly two weeks.

"I haven't been with anyone since Damian," Ashley confessed. She shifted, curling against him. "There were a few guys before I met him, but I was pretty young then. It didn't really count."

"You're still pretty young."

"Jeff!"

He looked at her as she raised herself up on one elbow. "I'm twenty-five. That's hardly a baby."

"I'm thirty-three."

"So what? That makes you an old man?"

He was older than she could know. He'd seen so much that no one should ever see.

She sighed and settled back against him. He could feel her bare breast pressing against his arm. "You make me crazy," she murmured. "You're not that old."

"If you say so."

"I do. Besides, that wasn't the point. Damian was the first man I'd ever been with, which makes you the second."

Her words stunned him. He heard them and turned them over in his brain without having a clue as to what to do with them.

"Ashley?"

"Yeah, yeah, I get it. More than you wanted to know."

"Why did you tell me?"

"Because…" She pressed her lips to his bare arm. "Because I want you to know that I think what we have is very special. I think *you're* special."

She thought they had something. A relationship? Was that possible? He wanted to tell her that he didn't know how, that he wasn't safe. That *this* wasn't safe. Not for either of them.

"I didn't want this," she continued. "Getting involved, I mean. Based on how you live your life, I'm guessing you didn't want it, either. Which means we should probably assume it's just hormones and that whatever it is will pass."

He risked looking at her and nearly lost himself in her beautiful eyes. "What didn't you want?"

She smiled. "The complication. The attraction. I spent yesterday being completely schizophrenic—bouncing between grinning like an idiot and promising myself I would end this immediately."

So she'd been feeling the same things he had. "If you planned on telling me it was over last night, the lace nightgown was a mixed message."

"I know." Her smile faded. "Jeff, neither of us wants this. The timing is bad, it's confusing. There are probably a hundred reasons to pretend it never happened, but that's not what I want."

"What do you want?"

She settled her head on his shoulder and closed her eyes. "To play it by ear. To enjoy my time with you without getting too personally involved or getting hurt."

Until it's time for me to leave.

She didn't say those last words, but he heard the message and knew she was correct. They could pretend for now. Pretend that they were allowed to be lovers and act like other people. But they both knew the truth. Eventually she would walk away from him because he could never give her what she needed and deserved. And he would let her go because to keep her in his world meant being distracted. One mistake on an assignment could easily be the end of him and the client.

"I need to keep my own room," she said. "So Maggie doesn't get confused. I don't want her to know about this. I thought I'd plan on heading back there before she wakes up."

She was talking about spending her nights with him. Of them being together in the same bed for hours at a time. Not just making love, but holding and touching and sleeping together. Longing filled him. A need to inhale the scent of her and be with her until the memories were so strong that he could never forget.

"So what do you think?" she asked. She opened her eyes and looked at him. "You haven't said what you want."

He knew this was all pretend, but it was more than he had ever had, so it was enough. "I want to make you happy," he said. "I want to do whatever you would like."

She grinned. "Really?"

He turned her onto her back and slid one thigh between hers. "Absolutely anything."

"How wonderful," she murmured. "I'll give you a list of requests tonight."

"Why don't we start right now?"

"Mommy, I found one!" Maggie squealed with delight, then held up a brightly colored yellow plastic egg. "Uncle Jeff, look!"

"How many is that?" he asked.

Maggie glanced into her basket. "Four," she said

with a reverence generally used by chronic shoppers at a twice-yearly sale.

Ashley smiled at her daughter and fought against an unexplained urge to cry. Her eyes began to burn and her throat tightened. She blinked rapidly until her wayward feelings were under control.

Her weakened emotional state was easy to explain, she thought as she sat next to Jeff on the rear step of his house. Ever since she was twelve years old, she'd been fighting to keep her world together. First she'd had to deal with her sister's death and the subsequent loss of her mother. Then she'd struggled to keep afloat in the foster home system. She'd managed to graduate from high school and start college, only to find herself in love with a charming loser who had no business being a husband let alone a father. Then she'd been a single mother, barely able to keep her world together.

For the past thirteen years, life had been one challenge after another. For the first time since the trouble all started, Ashley had a chance to relax and just breathe. Thanks to her job as Jeff's housekeeper and the part-time accounting work she did, she actually had a savings account. She was current in her studies, every day her graduation from college was that much closer, Maggie was happy and healthy and they had a very impressive roof over their heads.

All because of Jeff.

Ashley glanced at him out of the corner of her eye. He'd dressed for church in a beautiful navy suit, but she happened to know that shortly after six that morning, he'd been outside in jeans and a sweatshirt, hiding Easter eggs. He'd concealed them just enough that

Maggie wouldn't think the Easter bunny had gone soft on her, yet she was finding every single one of the plastic eggs.

Last night Jeff had helped Ashley prepare the eggs, filling the hollow plastic with chocolates, stickers and gaudy Day-Glo rings. He was growing on her; he was growing on them both.

Ashley recognized the danger signs. It wasn't just that Jeff made love to her every night with an attention to detail that left her breathless. Somehow the three of them had created rituals. Jeff and Maggie went grocery shopping twice a week. Fridays were movie-and-popcorn nights, complete with a rented Disney video and plenty of cuddling on the sofa. Jeff had watched Maggie two evenings before Ashley's last set of midterms.

He always asked about both their days, listening intently as if the information were essential to world peace. Or maybe it was just essential to his own well-being. He talked about work, explaining he had a business trip to the Mediterranean late the following month, and kept her updated on the performance of the new recruits.

"Six!" Maggie hollered as she held up another plastic egg.

Jeff stood. "Well done, young lady. Most impressive. As I believe the quota for each child is six eggs per Easter bunny visit, you've found them all."

"Really?" Maggie's blue eyes glowed with pride. "Mommy, I found them all!"

"You are a very clever little girl," Ashley said, holding out her arms to her daughter.

Maggie ran to her for a hug, then turned to Jeff

and held up her free arm. The tall, dangerous man bent low and scooped the child into his arms. Ashley's heart tightened in her chest. Both she and her daughter had it bad. Jeff no longer scared them, if he'd ever scared Maggie. He was kind and gentle and he paid attention. How was she supposed to resist him?

Jeff headed for the back door. Ashley rose and followed. He was so good with her daughter. How tragic that he couldn't have children of his own. He would be the best kind of father. Nicole had been wrong to tell him he wasn't human. Jeff Ritter was very much a man—as flawed and frail as the next. But he was also decent.

She stepped into the kitchen where Maggie and Jeff had already opened several of the plastic eggs to discover the goodies inside. Her daughter laughed with excitement over a bright orange ring in the shape of a daisy. She looked up at her mother and grinned.

"This is the bestest Easter ever. Can we go to church now, and then to Brenda's where I can see Muffin again?"

Ashley nodded and held out her hand. "Let's put on our Easter dresses and get all pretty for Uncle Jeff."

Maggie clasped her hands together in front of her chest. "We have hats," she said happily.

Jeff raised his eyebrows. Ashley smiled. "I know it's silly, but it's a tradition. New Easter hats."

"I can't wait to see them."

His gaze met hers. Ashley's heart squeezed a little tighter. In that moment she knew that she'd fallen for

Jeff. Fallen hard and fast with no hope of walking away without being crushed.

"Why is everyone staring?" Ashley asked in a low voice as they walked through Brenda's house in Bellevue.

Jeff had also noticed the interested looks they were receiving. He put his hand on the small of Ashley's back. "It's because you're so lovely."

She glanced up at him and laughed. "Yeah, right."

He took in her dark, wavy hair, the hazel eyes that seemed to see down to his soul, the way her mouth turned up slightly at the corners. She wore a cream-colored dress with long sleeves. The heavy fabric outlined her curves, falling gracefully to her calves. Atop her head sat a small scrap of lace and fabric that could only be called a hat under the loosest of interpretations. She looked beautiful and elegant and he couldn't believe they were here together.

"Maybe it's you," she murmured. "After all, you're not so bad looking yourself."

"I'm sure that's it."

She chuckled and took a glass of orange juice from a tray circulated by a tuxedo-clad waiter.

Brenda's house was spacious. Her husband had joined Microsoft in the days when the computer firm was little more than a start-up. Their wealth was reflected in the elegant furniture and attractive artwork. But while Ashley admired the decorator touches, Jeff counted exits and planned escape routes. He knew there was no point, but old habits died hard.

"So tell me about this brunch," Ashley said. "She goes all out."

"It's a yearly tradition." He glanced around the crowded living room. "Most of the employees from the security company are here, along with a lot of people from her husband's work. The rest are friends and family."

"Do you come often?"

"No."

He didn't bother to tell her that this was the first time he'd attended. That combined with him showing up with a gorgeous woman and her daughter explained all the attention they attracted, but he wasn't about to tell Ashley that, either. From what he could figure out, she thought of him as relatively normal. He didn't want to do anything to change her opinion before circumstances did it for him.

"Well, well, fancy seeing you here."

Jeff held in a groan. Fate hadn't taken long to burst his bubble, he thought as he turned to greet his partner.

Zane Rankin stood with a young woman clinging to his arm. She was in her early twenties, with long blond hair and a chest so large, it threatened her ability to stay upright. Her scrap of a dress barely covered her from breasts to thighs.

Jeff turned and shook hands with his partner, then introduced Ashley. Zane's date, Amee—"No *y* just a double *e*"—giggled.

"Zane says you're really dangerous, like him. That you could kill someone with your bare hands."

Jeff shot Zane a death look that was depressingly ineffective. "This isn't the sort of place I can demonstrate that," he said coldly.

"Oh." The young woman glanced around at the

crowd. "I guess not. It's Easter. I guess we have to be nice to each other today, you know?" She cuddled against Zane. "Maybe you can tell me about it later."

Zane leaned close her to ear. "Honey, I'll give you a personal tour of the vulnerable areas."

Amee giggled again. She disentangled her arm and touched Ashley's hand. "I have to go to the little girl's room. Want to come?"

Ashley shot Jeff a helpless look before following the other woman out of the living room. Jeff glared at his partner.

"Just once I'd like to see you with a woman whose IQ was slightly larger than her chest."

Zane grinned. "My normal response to that would be to say that I'd like to see you with a woman. But you're with one. I'm surprised, Jeff. And impressed. What you lack in quantity, you make up for in quality."

"Thank you."

Maggie raced toward him, a moplike ball of fur tagging along. "Uncle Jeff, Brenda said I can brush Muffin and we're going to watch a movie together."

She raised her arms as she approached and he automatically swept her up against his chest. Muffin raised herself up on her back feet, her front paws scrambling against his legs as if she, too, wanted to be picked up.

Zane raised his dark eyebrows. "Uncle Jeff, why don't you introduce me to this lovely young woman?"

Jeff would rather have left the brunch. Too many people were watching him, talking about the shock of seeing him with a child. He knew they were right,

that he had no business being with an innocent like
Maggie. But for reasons that weren't clear to him, the
little girl wasn't afraid. He hoped he didn't do anything to change that.

"This is Maggie," he said. "Ashley's daughter
Maggie, this is Zane Rankin. I work with him."

Maggie's blue eyes widened. "Uncle Jeff is very
important. He keeps bad men away. Do you do that
too?"

"Sure," Zane said easily. "But Uncle Jeff is the
best."

Maggie snuggled close to him. "I know." She
pressed her tiny rosebud mouth against his cheek,
then motioned for him to put her down. "Muffin really wants to see the movie," she explained, gave him
a quick wave, then disappeared into the crowd.

As soon as they were alone, Zane's gaze turned
speculative. "I hadn't realized you and the kid were
so close."

Jeff shrugged. "She's pretty easy to like."

What he didn't say was that Maggie terrified him.
He didn't want to do anything to hurt her and the
knowledge that he could was just one more thing that
kept him up nights.

Zane looked as if he wanted to say something else,
but then he stepped back. "The ladies have returned."

Jeff turned and saw Ashley and Amee approaching.
Zane was watching them, as well, but Jeff noticed his
friend was paying as much attention to Ashley as to
his own date.

Something hot flared to life inside of his chest. It
took him a moment to recognize the bitter heat of

jealousy. No way, he told himself. Jealous of Zane? Ashley hadn't looked twice at the man. Besides, Zane would never try anything. Ashley wasn't his type. But despite the logic, the feeling remained, making him uncomfortably aware of being out of his element.

He wasn't prepared to be a part of society's mainstream, he reminded himself. The cries of the dead were never quiet and he would do well to remember that.

"Amee was telling me the most interesting things about your business," Ashley said as she stepped close to him. "Did you and Zane really single-handedly save the British royal family from certain death?"

Jeff shot Zane a questioning look. His partner grinned. "Okay, so I might have exaggerated the story a little."

Ashley moved close to Jeff. "How much? I want to hear the part where you threw yourself on the queen to save her from a flying bullet."

Amee beamed. "Aren't they just the bravest men? Zane has over a dozen scars. You should see them."

"Maybe another time," Ashley murmured.

Jeff looked into her eyes and saw the humor lurking there. "There was no incident involving the royal family," he said softly into her ear. "They have their own security."

"I figured as much, but Amee was so proud."

They watched as the blond bombshell ran her manicured fingers up Zane's arm. "Zane's offered to show me what he does," the young woman said, "but I'd be too frightened."

"You mean, take you on an assignment?" Ashley asked, sounding doubtful.

"No. They have an executive training course in a couple of weeks." Amee sighed. "But it's just too scary for me."

Zane winked at Ashley. "Maybe you'd like to go. It's just for a weekend. You could check out what it is Jeff does with his day."

Jeff hesitated. His first instinct was to change the subject. No way did he want Ashley to see what he did in his world. She would be terrified. Which meant it probably wasn't a bad idea. Her being scared would be the safest way to end the relationship before he did something stupid and hurt her. Her current view of him wasn't based in reality. The weekend away would change that.

"I'm intrigued," Ashley admitted. "What happens during the training weekend?"

Zane shrugged. "It's no big deal. A dozen or so executives join us in the mountains. We have a special resort we use. It's rustic, but not unpleasantly so. We teach them some basics about staying safe, how to recognize a terrorist threat, that sort of thing."

"Why do I think it's slightly more complicated than that?" Ashley asked.

"You'd be perfectly safe," Jeff assured her. "If you're interested, I'm sure Brenda would be willing to baby-sit."

She stared at him. "Do you want me go?"

No, he didn't. But he also knew it was important that she saw a piece of his reality. Being around her was changing him, and not for the better. He was getting weaker, softer. If she saw the truth, she would back off.

"I think you'd find it interesting," he said. "There's nothing dangerous for the participants. It's not survival training."

"Are there bugs?"

He grinned. "Just little ones. You could take them."

"Okay. Sounds like fun. If Brenda doesn't mind watching Maggie, I'll go."

"Great." Zane gave her a thumbs-up. "I'll arrange everything."

Just then Brenda announced that brunch was being served in the main dining room. Jeff put his hand on the small of Ashley's back and ushered her toward the doorway. Amee said something about shoes and the subject was changed. But he couldn't stop thinking about the weekend retreat, two short weeks away. Nothing would be the same at the end of those forty-eight hours. He wasn't sure if his friend had done him a favor or just sent him a one-way ticket to hell.

Chapter Twelve

The site of the executive security camp was a lodge on the east side of the Cascade Mountains. As always, the weather was better than on the Seattle side. Ashley stepped into sunshine as she exited Jeff's BMW.

"Now here's something I haven't seen in a while," she joked as she raised her face to the warm rays.

The past few weeks had been typical for spring in Seattle. Plenty of cool days and lots of rain. The weather people kept hinting at sunshine but then changing the forecast.

Her feet crunched on the gravel parking lot as she moved to the rear of Jeff's car and waited for him to open the trunk. She glanced at the cars around them. "Lexus, Jaguars, Mercedes and..." she counted "three limos. So, Jeff, tell me about these clients of yours."

He pulled her shabby suitcase from the cavernous truck. His own bag was soft, black leather. It was so smooth to the touch, she wouldn't mind a coat in the same material.

"Executives," he said. "I told you that."

"Yeah, but I was thinking about my local bank branch manager. These people are way different."

He grinned. "I think one of our participants might own your bank. That counts."

"Oh, sure. We can have a detailed conversation about the way the ATMs seem to always go out at five o'clock on Fridays."

She looked at the lodge, noticing for the first time that it seemed much more elegant than rustic. She returned her attention to Jeff and realized he was dressed in one of his tailored suits. Why did she suddenly have a bad feeling that she was completely out of her element?

"Jeff, maybe I don't belong here."

He set his bag on the ground, then draped an arm around her. "Don't be nervous. You have as much right to be here as anyone else. They're all going to feel just as awkward because they're all out of place. This is combat, not the board room. My staff and I make sure everyone attending is clear on who are the experts."

She leaned into him, inhaling the familiar scent of his body. "Like that's making me feel better." She felt his mouth brush against the top of her head. Which did ease some of her tension. "So why are you in a suit?" she asked. "You told me to dress casual."

He had, in fact, insisted on jeans, sweatshirts and

boots or athletic shoes. The sky might be a whole lot clearer on this side of the mountain, but the air temperature wasn't much warmer.

"I have to impress the clients during the introductory session. If I dress like them, they'll relax."

"So later you'll show up in your soldier's clothes?"

"I promise."

She glanced up at him and grinned. "Can I swoon?"

"Do you want to?"

"With every breath I take."

"Liar," he murmured, then kissed her briefly before releasing her and grabbing her suitcase as well as his own.

She followed him into the lodge.

The main room was huge, both wide and tall, soaring up three stories. On the far wall was a fireplace large enough to host a committee meeting. There was plenty of wood and trophy heads mounted on the wall. The reception desk stretched for about fifty feet. It was midafternoon on a Friday and the place should have been crowded. Instead she saw only one other guest. Jeff had told her they rented the entire place even though their client list was kept at less than twenty-five. She couldn't imagine what the executives were spending on the three-day course. Although if the information kept them alive, how could they put a price on the weekend?

This was Jeff's world and she was about to get an inside view of it. She couldn't decide if that was good or bad. Maybe—

Jeff stopped just short of the reception desk and

turned to her. "What did you want to do about a room?" he asked.

Ashley blinked. "A room? I'd prefer to have one. Sleeping in the car has never been my idea of a good time."

"Did you want one of your own?"

It took her a second to figure out what he was asking. A room of her own, as in did she want them to share a room?

"We're not at home," he continued, avoiding her gaze, which was so unlike Jeff. "I thought you might prefer to have the privacy."

He was nervous, she thought suddenly. And embarrassed, if his shuffling feet were anything to go by. She wouldn't have thought Jeff capable of either emotion.

"Will I be in the way if I stay with you?"

His gray gaze settled on her face. His look was so intense, it was almost like being touched by him.

"I'd prefer us to be together," he said, "but it's your call."

She raised herself on tiptoes. "Do you think they have a room with a mirror on the ceiling?"

He grinned. "I'll ask."

He moved to the reception desk. As he registered them, Ashley felt a fluttering sensation in the center of her chest. A warm, mushy kind of fluttering that occurred more and more when she was with Jeff. She knew what it meant and it scared her to death. She did *not* want to be falling for this man. Especially when she didn't know what he was feeling about her. She wanted to think that this mattered to him, that it was more than just casual, but she couldn't be sure.

"Ready?" he asked.

"What?"

She glanced around and saw that their bags had been whisked away. He handed her a room key, then put his hand on the small of her back to urge her forward. They walked down a long corridor that led to the conference rooms. Double doors stood open. A young woman smiled and handed Jeff a clipboard and Ashley a name tag. Only her first name had been printed in block letters.

"Let's go," he said, and motioned for her to step into the conference room. Ashley prayed for courage, then did as he requested.

The room was about forty by forty, with several conference tables set up, facing front. About two dozen people stood talking in small groups. There were only two other women and they were both older than Ashley by at least a decade.

All the name tags had first names only, with no indication of who was whom or where anyone was from. She noticed several of Jeff's staff standing around the perimeter of the room. Zane was up in front, talking with one of the hotel staff. When he saw Jeff, he shook hands with the staff member and moved toward his partner. Ashley took a seat at the end of one of the tables. No one might be identified by location and occupation, but she could tell that everyone here was wealthy, powerful and probably tipped more than she made in a year. Why on earth had she let herself be talked into this?

"Welcome," Jeff said as he moved to the front of the room. "Ritter/Rankin Security is pleased to have you here for our executive security weekend retreat. I'm Jeff Ritter and this is my partner, Zane Rankin.''

Everyone took a seat. A short, round man sat next to Ashley. He appeared to be close to sixty and had the most gorgeous diamond pinky ring she'd ever seen. His suit looked softer than her flannel pj's and she would swear she'd seen his face in the international financial section of the Seattle paper. Please God, don't let him want to exchange business cards, she thought humorously.

''One of our staff members is moving among you, passing out a schedule for the weekend,'' Jeff continued.

Ashley took the offered notebook and opened it.

''We're here to teach you about being safe,'' Jeff went on. ''In one afternoon and two days, you're not going to become experts. That's not our goal. What we want to teach you is preparedness and awareness. You need to know what kind of security you're going to need so you can hire the best available.

''The first lecture is on security preparation. We'll touch on various dangers, what is likely and what is unlikely to happen to you when you travel. We'll talk about threats to your family. We will also discuss the duties and responsibilities of a security detail.

''Later this afternoon we'll have our first session on weapons. This will occur at the firing range away from the lodge. You'll be handling everything from a handgun to a submachine gun.

''Saturday morning we'll focus on terrorist threats. Who, where, how and when. This will include information on both bombs and booby traps. Saturday afternoon is evasive driving.

"On Sunday everyone will participate in three different mock terrorist situations. The goal is to make you aware and cautious. If that means putting the fear of God into each and every one of you, all the better. Nobody dies on my watch. Any questions?"

Ashley had to consciously keep from letting her mouth drop open. She thought about all the time she'd spent with him and how they laughed and talked and made love late into the night. She was having trouble reconciling that man with the man in front of her. She'd wanted a chance to find out about Jeff's world. Now that she was here, it was a little late to be having second thoughts.

"When in doubt, trust no one," Zane said later that afternoon as he paced the length of the conference room. He pointed to a man in the front row. "John, tell me a bit about your business."

The man, a forty-something British executive, adjusted the front of his khaki-colored shirt and cleared his throat. "The company is a multinational software conglomerate. We have—"

"Any kids?" Zane asked, interrupting.

"Yes, three. Two boys and a girl."

"Any of them away at school?"

"One son is at Eton."

"You must be proud."

"I am. Margaret and I—"

"Margaret's your wife?"

"Yes. She and I have been most fortunate in that our children are..."

John's voice trailed off when he realized one of the security staff was typing into a portable computer.

Seconds later the printer shot out several pieces of paper.

"What is going on here?" he demanded, rising to his feet.

Zane took the pages and handed them to him. Then he turned his attention to the group. "John just gave the lives of his wife and children to a terrorist group determined to make its mark. In the time it took him to share some general information about his occupation, the type of company he worked for, the name of his wife and the number of his children, we were able to pull together a relatively complete file on him. The data bank already exists. Incomplete profiles are stored and as more details are learned, the profiles grow. One slip—a son in Eton, the name of a spouse—can bring it all together."

John flipped through the pages and swore softly. "I didn't know."

"Most people don't. You got off lightly this time. We've screened everyone. No lurking terrorists. Next time you might not be so lucky." He pointed to John's name tag. "That's why first names only." Zane turned to Ashley. "Tell us about yourself."

She couldn't help smiling. "I don't think I know you well enough to share any details. But thanks for asking."

"Exactly right," Zane said, winking at her. "Better to be considered rude than be found dead. Remember, if you don't know the person, don't take the risk. It's not worth it." He glanced at his watch and nodded at Jeff. "Let's switch subjects. If you'll turn to the next section in your notebooks."

"Security," Jeff said by way of introduction.

"Having too much staff is just as useless as having too little. Don't get caught up in the game of looking good with an entourage."

He continued talking, but Ashley wasn't paying attention to his words. She was too mesmerized by how he looked. She took in the fatigues, the baseball-style military cap, the gun strapped to his waist. He was a stranger—a very exciting, very dangerous-looking stranger. He was—

Both sets of side doors burst open and nearly a dozen armed, masked men poured into the room. Someone screamed. Ashley thought it might have been her, but her throat was too dry. Her heart leaped into her throat, making it impossible to breathe.

Before she knew what was happening, the men were grabbing people and forcing them toward the rear of the room. Everything happened so quickly. There was a gunshot and a cry. Instinctively she turned to catch sight of Jeff. At first she couldn't see where he was but then she noticed him by the front wall. He was checking his watch.

She felt someone grab her arm and roughly thrust her toward the rear of the room. Seconds later a voice yelled, "Clear!"

Jeff looked up. "Thirty-two seconds. That's how long it took my men to collect you into an easily manageable group. Give them another twenty-five seconds and you'd all be dead."

The man who had been "shot" scrambled to his feet. He was one of the security staff. He patted his chest and grinned. "Blanks on a bulletproof vest. I didn't feel a thing."

"Now that I have your attention," Jeff said, "let's

talk about buying the best. Don't be cheap. Get the best people and give them the most dependable equipment available. Newer isn't always better. Figuring out what they should have isn't your job—you have experts for that. But don't skimp. Yes, a clip that holds more bullets costs more. So what? Isn't your life worth that?''

He put down his clipboard. ''Let's take a fifteen-minute break so that your heart rates can get back to normal.''

Ashley pressed her hand to her chest and wondered if that would ever happen. At least her heart had returned to her chest. She moved over to the table set up with sodas and water. She opened a can of a diet drink and sipped. A few of the other participants chatted to each other while most pulled out their cell phones and made calls.

Zane walked over to where she stood and he grinned. ''Great huh? Did you ever feel so alive?''

''Yes,'' she said. ''I felt very alive before I thought I was going to die. That was not my idea of a good time.''

Zane laughed as he moved away, but she didn't think it was funny. She turned her attention to Jeff who was busy answering questions. For the first time she was starting to understand who and what he was. A warrior.

She remembered he'd told her Nicole had said he wasn't human. Ashley disagreed. He was very human. He was just better trained and more willing to die than most people. He was also very special. How many men like him would be willing to take the time to braid a little girl's hair or read her a story? How many would bother with things like Easter egg hunts or remember to compliment her on a new hat?

Yes, he was a warrior and she loved him.

Ashley closed her eyes against the sudden burning behind her lids. She didn't want to start crying here, but emotion overwhelmed her. She loved Jeff. It was a thousand kinds of stupid and yet she hadn't been able to stop herself.

To make matters worse, along with the love came fear. She knew what she wanted in her life—someone who would love her completely, more than he'd ever loved anyone else ever. She desperately needed to be first in his life.

Was that Jeff? Did he care about her that way? She wanted to believe it was possible, but she wasn't sure. Could the warrior open himself that much? His life was so different from hers. She couldn't go where he went. Would he be willing to stay on her side of the line?

She felt a hand on her shoulder, turned and saw Jeff standing next to her.

"Are you all right?" he asked, concern deepening his voice.

She forced herself to smile. "Zane seemed to feel it was all a joke, designed to make us feel alive. I told him I was plenty alive enough before. If anything, the attack scared about three years of life out of me."

"That's the adrenaline. It's a powerful chemical, but it will fade."

She touched her chest. "So I'll be able to breathe without gasping?"

"Just give it a minute." He brushed his fingers

against her cheek. "How are you holding up? Any regrets?"

"About four dozen, but I'm still enjoying myself. It's really different from my ordinary life."

"Are you surprised?"

"By the differences? No." she shrugged. "I knew what you did, but I never understood the details. There are way too many ways to kill people."

"My job is to make sure that doesn't happen."

"Agreed, but is it what you do or who you are?"

She knew what she wanted him to say. Unfortunately she also knew what he was going to say.

"It's who I am," he told her. "That can't change."

"I know," she said with a lightness she didn't feel. "But a girl can dream."

He dropped his hand to his side. His gaze grew more intense. "What do you dream about, Ashley? What do you want?"

She wanted him to be different. To be an ordinary man who worked in a bank or a factory. She didn't want someone who saved the world because causes were often so much more important than people. She wanted him to be the kind of man who would love her back.

She was as foolish as a child crying for the moon.

"Pizza," she said at last. "The all-meat kind with sausage and pepperoni. What do think? Is there a take-out pizza place around here?"

At first she didn't think he was going to let her change the subject. But she suspected Jeff didn't want to discuss their differences any more than she did.

"I happen to know a great little place in town. We'll have it delivered."

"Sounds perfect." She turned away, then glanced at him over her shoulder. "And while we're waiting we can take a bath...together."

"I've never been much for speeding," Ashley said uneasily the next afternoon. She eyed the souped-up dark town car parked in front of her, then glanced at the oval course laid out in a field about ten miles from the lodge.

The sealed concrete road went straight for about a quarter mile before curving through a series of turns. It disappeared behind a screen of trees, but she knew that on the far side of the track someone was spraying the surface with a slick mixture designed to make the tires slip. Assuming she survived that, the next section of the course would include an ambush, complete with gunshots and explosions. Being a passenger had been harrowing enough. Now it was her turn to drive.

She understood the point of the exercise. The people who took this course for real were powerful enough to be kidnapping targets. Should that happen on the road, they had to be prepared. This afternoon wouldn't substitute for a professional driving course, but it was an introduction. Ashley tried to find humor in the situation by wondering if the training would help her get a better parking place at the grocery store.

Zane patted her back. "You don't get special concession just because you're female."

She glared at him. "Did I ask for any?"

He shrugged. "You look kinda whiny."

She planted her hands on her hips. "Do you think annoying me is going to make me drive better?"

"It'll keep you from being nervous."

Jeff strolled over and glanced down at the list on his clipboard. "Ashley, you're up next as the driver. Are you ready?"

"Only if I get to kill Zane when I get back."

Jeff chuckled. "Is he getting on your nerves?"

"Like nails on a chalkboard."

"Were you scared?"

She looked at the big car and then at the course. "Maybe."

"So it worked."

She sighed. "I hate it when you two act all superior just because you're professional soldiers."

Jeff opened the driver's door and reached inside for the safety helmet. "Relax, concentrate and drive fast."

"Can I do just two out of three?" she asked.

"No. All three are required."

Grumbling under her breath, she fastened on the helmet, then slid behind the wheel of the town car. Two men, bankers from New York, got into the rear. Zane rode shotgun. Jeff stood at the side of the track with a clipboard in one hand and a stopwatch in the other.

"Whenever you're ready," he called.

Ashley nodded. She took a deep breath to try to ease the tension in her body. It didn't work. She wiped her damp palms on her jeans and tried to tell herself that this was just pretend. Nothing bad was going to happen. Except she knew that it could. One of the participants had overturned the other town car an hour before. No one had been hurt but the car had been totaled.

She glanced at her passengers. ''Helmets on, gen tlemen,'' she said.

When everyone was safely buckled in, she starte the car and drove onto the track.

The purpose of the exercise was to feel what it wa like to have to drive evasively. They'd all seen video on the subject and watched a demonstration Now they were being given a chance to practice it fo themselves.

Based on the way the cars had fishtailed all ove the road, Ashley knew she was in for a challenge.

''You're driving like a girl,'' Zane said blandly a she eased into the first curve.

She didn't bother looking at him. ''This kind c strategy may work on your recruits,'' she said, ''bu as I am a girl, it doesn't do a thing for me.''

As she left the first curve, she accelerated. The ex ercise was timed, but she would lose points for ski ding off the road.

There were three *S* curves in succession, then long straight section. At the end of it, the concret glistened from the slick substance she would have pass over. Gritting her teeth, Ashley floored the ca then eased up as they approached the oily mixture She barely touched the steering wheel, so as not t change the direction of the car.

The vehicle moved straight for the first twenty fee then began to slide off the road. Ashley had watche the other drivers try to fight with the car. Instead sh guided it to the side of the road. Once they settle onto the dirt shoulder, she pressed on the accelerato The tires had traction and she was able to steer aroun the last of the slick trap.

Only when she was back on the road did she risk glancing at Zane. He didn't react at all. "Not bad," he murmured.

Ashley allowed herself a grin. She knew she'd done a whole lot better than not bad. She was about to tell him so when gunfire exploded all around the car.

"Get down," she yelled.

A smaller vehicle pulled out next to her and moved close, trying to crowd her off the road.

She ignored the gunfire and the other car, instead concentrating on the track in front of her. She gunned the engine, shooting forward. There was an explosion off to her right, but Ashley ignored it. Another car came up on her right. She swung her car toward it, bashing it once, then sped off toward the finish line.

It was only when she'd stopped the car that she realized her heart was racing. She'd done it! She'd completed the course.

"What's my time?" she asked Zane.

"Three seconds behind Henry's."

"Three seconds?" She jumped out of the car and practically danced to where Jeff was standing with a clipboard of his own. "I'm right behind Henry. In second place."

"I know," he said without looking at her.

She slapped the back of her hand against his upper arm. "Come on." She leaned close. "Admit it. You think I'm pretty hot stuff."

He looked up. She saw the pride and affection in his eyes. "I'm more impressed than you know."

Chapter Thirteen

A sharp cry cut through the night. Ashley's first thought was that this was yet another trick of Jeff's staff at the executive retreat. But when she opened her eyes, she recognized Jeff's bedroom in his large house on Queen Anne Hill. This wasn't a drill.

She blinked in the darkness and tried to figure out what she'd heard. Was Maggie having a bad dream? Her daughter didn't usually—

The cry came again, but not from down the hall. Instead, the sharp outburst of pain came from the man lying next to her. Ashley turned toward Jeff. As she did so, she glanced at the clock and saw that it was nearly two in the morning. Often she returned to her own bed to sleep, but tonight something had compelled her to stay with Jeff. Now, as she watched him fight with the covers and speak harsh, unintelligible phrases, she was glad she was there for him.

She reached out to touch his arm, then remembered the weekend they'd just spent together. He was very much a warrior. While she'd had clues about his skills before, now she had firsthand knowledge. She wanted to wake him up without finding herself in some kind of death grip. She knew he wouldn't deliberately hurt her, but she had no idea of the content of his dream. In the second or two it took him to return to reality, he could do a lot of damage.

So instead of touching him, she turned on the light sitting on the nightstand and softly spoke his name.

He came awake instantly. His eyes opened and he made a quick, visual search of the room. When his gaze settled on her, he stiffened.

"I was dreaming."

She nodded. "You cried out. Are you all right?"

It was only as she spoke the words that she realized he was both sweaty and ashen. The sound of his harsh breathing seemed to fill the room.

"Jeff? What's wrong?"

"Nothing. I'm fine."

He was anything but. She nibbled on her lower lip, not sure what to do with him. She couldn't force him to talk nor could she physically make him relax. Not knowing what else to do, she left the light on, but slid back under the covers and snuggled close to him. She lay with her head on her pillow but her arm across his chest. She pressed her legs against his and waited.

Slowly he began to relax. His breathing evened out and his heated body cooled. While she'd slipped on a nightgown after they'd finished making love, Jeff was still naked. She ran her fingers through the hair on his chest, pausing when she felt a long, slender scar running the length of his rib cage.

"What is this from?"

"A knife fight."

"Where'd you get it?"

"Afghanistan."

She frowned. "I don't remember us sending troops into..." Her voice trailed off. "Oh. I guess I wasn't supposed to know."

"No."

She sighed. "Jeff, was it like the dream you told me about before? The one where the village is burning and the people are running from you?"

"Yes."

He wasn't being overly chatty. "There's more to it, though, isn't there? You've had the dream before when I was with you and I don't remember you crying out."

He half turned away.

She raised herself up on one elbow and touched his cheek. "Jeff? You can tell me. I'm not afraid of you. If this is a privacy issue, that's one thing, but if it's about protecting me, I'll have to slap you."

Her last comment made him turn back to her. He smiled slightly. "Zane told me you were offended by all his 'girl' comments. I have to remember to inform him you don't take a lot of guff from anyone."

"That's right. I've had natural childbirth. I know about suffering. I don't think you can say anything to shock me. So if you want to talk, I'm happy to listen."

His smile faded and he closed his eyes. "It was a

different dream," he said quietly. "A visitation from the souls of the dead."

At first she didn't understand what he was saying. And then she knew. The souls of the dead were from people he had killed. She settled back on the bed, resting her head on his shoulder.

"You were a soldier. You did what you were told."

"Does that make it right?"

"I don't know. I do know that it doesn't make you a monster. Despite your ex-wife's claims to the contrary, you're not inhuman."

He swallowed. "Maggie was there. In my dream. She was screaming for me to save her and I couldn't. Every time I got close enough to reach her, she saw me and ran away."

Ashley shuddered. She didn't want to hear any more. She didn't want to know what Jeff had suffered in the process of defending his country and doing his job. She wished there were a way to heal him.

"There's a psychological reason that Maggie has suddenly appeared in your dreams," she said. "You care about her and you want to keep her safe. I have a friend who has a recurring dream about losing a baby. Her kids are long grown and gone, but that doesn't ease the worrying."

"Knowing that doesn't make it any less real in the dream."

"I know." She pressed a kiss to his shoulder. "Jeff, I'm really willing to listen if you think it will help."

He didn't answer. She continued to hold him close. Eventually his eyes fluttered shut and she thought he might have gone back to sleep. She hoped so. He needed his rest. But after a time, he started speaking.

"I can't tell you anything more," he said. "I would never do that. If you knew the truth, you'd never be able to close your eyes again."

At first she didn't believe him, but then he turned to face her and she saw the truth of his words in his expression. She remembered all he'd talked about over the recent weekend. The lessons, the casually told stories. The professional attitude of a man who knows his subject. Suddenly she was cold. A shiver passed through her. She didn't want to know the horrors of his past.

Without meaning to, she recalled a lecture from the weekend. It had been about bombs and booby traps, and the damage they could do on the human body. Jeff's knowledge didn't come from a book; it came from experience. From watching people die. There had been so much horror and Jeff had been caught in the middle of it.

"I so want to make it better," she breathed, and touched his cheek. "Jeff, I don't know how."

He took her hand and pressed his mouth to her palm. In that moment, every last doubt she'd ever had faded as if it had never been. She was more sure than ever that she loved him. She'd probably loved him from the first. It didn't matter how he felt about her, if he loved her or not. He owned her, heart and soul.

"Why are you crying?" he asked, his voice a whisper.

She sniffed. "I didn't realize I was."

He brushed tears from her face. "Why?"

What's wrong? I've been thinking about the sequence of events in recent days. As near as I can figure it, you started acting weird last Monday. Which means it was after that dream you had. The one we talked about. What's the problem, Jeff? Did we connect? Are you concerned because I'm getting too close?"

She was, but not in the way she meant. He was waiting for her to figure out the truth about him and then run.

She sighed. "What is it? Are you mad at me?"

"No. Of course not."

"Oooh, he speaks." She glared. "Okay, you're not mad. What about having Maggie and me here. Are you changing your mind about that?"

Her question stunned him. He half rose to his feet before settling back in his leather chair. "I don't want you to move out. I enjoy having you here."

She took another step closer to the desk. "Finally we're getting somewhere. Okay, so you're not mad and you want us here. Are you happy?"

He wasn't even sure what she meant, let alone figuring out the emotion itself.

"I can see from your face that you're not," she said with a sigh, and settled into the chair opposite his desk. "Okay. Not mad, not happy, yet you still want me here. Care to explain all this?"

She was trying. He could tell that he'd confused her and he needed to make things more clear. The problem was he didn't know how.

"It's about the dream," he told her, staring at the desk, not wanting to see her expression. "I don't like that I have it. I don't like what it says."

"You mean you're uncomfortable about your past?"

"No." He sucked in a breath. "You saw my weak spot."

When she didn't say anything, he looked at her. She stared at him blankly. He nearly groaned. How much more was he supposed to explain? Why didn't she get it? Weakness was danger. Weakness was to be despised. He wanted to be with her and he was terrified of her getting too close. He was a soldier and he needed a soldier's detachment. When he was around her, he couldn't stay detached. Not anymore.

For the first time in his life he was afraid. Of what was inside of him. Of losing someone important.

She leaned toward him and rested her arms on his desk. "Was the weakness that you shared it with me or was it what you talked about?"

"What we discussed."

She stared at him. "Okay. We talked about the dream and your inability to rescue Maggie. Is it that you failed?"

He shifted in his seat. Was she torturing him on purpose? "Yes."

"Are you afraid I'll use your perceived weakness against you or think less of you?"

He sprang to his feet. "Dammit, what else would it be?" he demanded.

She rose and glared at him. "Don't you yell at me. I'm not the idiot in this room. You are." She circled around the desk and pushed in front of him.

"I'm not the enemy," she said as she poked a finger into his chest. "Stop treating me like I am. Stop hiding out because you act like a human being. It's more than allowed. It's the sort of behavior I would encourage.''

She placed her hands on his arms and tried to shake him. "Don't you get it? I care about you." She paused as if she wanted to say more, then continued. "I won't hurt you. I won't think less of you. In fact, I admire you very much. Maybe in soldier-speak you've violated some manly code. Maybe in that world, showing your softer side is dangerous. But when it comes to a personal relationship between a man and a woman, being vulnerable is generally a good thing. I want you to trust me the way I trust you."

"You trust me?"

She threw up her hands. "Is that *all* you got out of what I said?"

"No."

He'd heard every word; he just wasn't sure he believed it.

"Jeff, here's the news flash, so pay attention. I care about you *more* because of your confession. Knowing about your pain and the darkness in your soul makes me feel closer to you. It doesn't make me want to run away. So if that was your goal, you failed."

His throat was dry and it was difficult to speak. "What about the weekend? Did that change anything?"

"Zane got on my nerves a little, but aside from that, no, nothing is different." She paused and looked up at him. "I take that back. I think I have a clearer understanding of what it is that you do. I respect your abilities more. But that's it."

He felt as if someone had lifted the weight of the

world off his shoulders. She wasn't mad, she wasn't running away.

"I'm glad," he said simply.

She smiled. "Prove it."

At first he wasn't sure what she meant. Then he saw the passion flaring in her eyes. She wanted him. She wanted to make love and have him touch her everywhere.

He didn't know how that was possible, but he wasn't about to ask questions or turn her down. Instead he wrapped his arms around her and picked her up until he could set her on the edge of the desk. Then he dropped his mouth to hers and kissed her.

By now he was familiar with the taste of her mouth. He slipped between her lips, savoring the soft sweetness waiting there. They touched and circled, performing a dance that was uniquely their own. Need filled him—a growing heat and desire that made his blood throb and that most male part of him flex against her belly.

She was perfect for him, he thought hazily as he broke the kiss and pressed his mouth to her jaw, then her neck. Everything about her was exactly right. The texture of her skin, the scent of her body, the way her hands rubbed against his chest, igniting fires before fumbling with his shirt buttons.

He grasped the hem of her sweater and tugged upward. She leaned back enough to allow him to pull the garment over her head and toss it to the floor. Her bra was next. He quickly unfastened the slender hook and slid the scrap of lace down her arms.

Her nipples were already tight buds, thrusting toward him in the faint coolness of the room. He cupped her breasts, absorbing their weight, their temperature and their silky smoothness. Need hummed hotter inside of him. He longed to rip the rest of her clothes from her body and thrust himself inside of her. But he held back. Giving Ashley pleasure first made his own release better. Not only was she slick and ready for him, he'd learned that once she climaxed, she would release again and again when he entered her. Those rapid contractions were the best part of making love with her.

He lowered his head and took her right nipple in his mouth. As he swirled his tongue around the beaded flesh, he settled his hands on her waist and began unfastening her jeans. Her fingers tangled themselves in his hair. She arched into his licking caresses, breathing heavily and murmuring his name.

With one quick tug, he shoved off her jeans and panties. She wore only socks scrunched around her ankles. The sight of her in them and nothing else was oddly erotic, so he left the socks in place. He shrugged out of his shirt and placed it on the desk behind her.

"Lie down," he instructed. "It's time I went to work."

She laughed even as she stretched out on the desk. He settled into his chair and pulled it close to her. She'd parted her legs and now he moved between them. He could already feel the heat of her arousal. She would be damp and ready for him. He knew exactly how sweet she would taste, how she would moan at the first stroke of his tongue, how her muscles would tense and her legs would draw back as she approached her climax.

Just thinking about how it would be made his own arousal tense painfully. Pressure throbbed at the base of his groin, but he ignored the sensation. There would be time for him later. Now he wanted to concentrate on Ashley.

He rested his hands on her belly and slid them up her body as he moved closer. As his fingers tickled her ribs, he nibbled his way up her thighs. First one side, then the other. Licking, kissing, biting gently. She gasped and giggled and breathed his name. Her hands settled on top of his, urging him higher until his palms settled on her breasts.

She shifted so that she could rest her feet on the arms of his chair, opening herself for him. He accepted the silent invitation and slowly licked her most feminine place. She gasped in pleasure. Her thighs parted more. He explored all of her, the place he would enter later, the sweet mysteries of her desire, before kissing that one spot designed to make her moan.

He found it easily, and knew exactly what to do. As his fingers toyed with her tight nipples, his tongue circled her center, moving over and around, teasing, rubbing, kissing, licking. He moved fast, then slow. He made her moan and then he made her beg. Only when her legs were trembling and her body slick with sweat did he give in to her demands and move in the steady rhythm designed to make her fall into ecstasy.

It took less than ten seconds. He licked her over and over, guiding her to her release. Then she shuddered in his intimate embrace. Her body quivered as her insides spasmed.

He held back as long as he could, waiting until she

had finally stilled. Only then did he stand and reach for his belt. He fumbled with the zipper before finally unfastening it. As he shoved down his pants, he pushed the chair out of the way and urged her to wrap her legs around his waist. Bracing his hands on the desk, he stared into her beautiful face and plunged into her.

One deep, slow thrust that had them both gasping. She clamped her muscles around him and smiled. Her eyes were still glazed with the lingering aftershocks of her release. As he moved in and out of her, he watched her expression tighten. At the same time he felt her body convulse around his. She moaned. He swallowed hard and struggled for self-control.

She didn't make it easy. He knew that as long as he moved in and out of her, she would climax, rippling against him, drawing him in deeper, forcing him over the edge. He pulsed his hips, then swore, knowing it wasn't supposed to be this good and never wanting it to stop.

Wait, he told himself. Hold back. But he couldn't. Using her legs, she pulled him closer, sending him in deeper, then gave herself up to the release. As she breathed his name, he felt himself losing control. He grasped her hips and pumped hard and fast. The sound of his blood rushing through his body filled his ears. He couldn't think, couldn't breathe, couldn't do anything but feel the intense release as he spilled himself into her.

When he'd recovered, he bent over her and kissed her mouth.

"Amazing as always," she said with a sigh. "You are a man of many talents."

He touched her cheeks, her nose, then her lower lip. "I aim to please."

"You reduce me to a puddle. That's more than pleasing." Her hazel eyes darkened. "No more hiding away, okay?"

He couldn't deny her anything. Even when it made sense to do so. "I promise."

Jeff typed in his notes on the report the team had prepared. They were getting close to finishing up the security plan for Kirkman and his associates. The meeting was in several days.

His phone rang and he took the call, but when he was finished, he found it difficult to return to his report. He wasn't concentrating very well these days. Ashley was always on his mind.

It had been nearly a week since she'd accused him of hiding out. A week during which their relationship continued to complicate his life. He knew that he should give her up but he couldn't seem to find the words to tell her goodbye. While being disconnected was the safest course of action, he found himself resisting returning to his solitary world. He enjoyed the warmth and the laughter Ashley and Maggie brought to his life. He enjoyed the passion Ashley brought to his bed. He liked knowing she was home, waiting for him, thinking about him. He trusted her.

While he'd trusted men with his life on a mission, he'd never trusted a woman before. Not with his heart and soul. He could almost imagine himself doing that with Ashley.

There were times when he wondered what was going to happen. How would he survive her walking away? He thought that—

The door to his office flew open and Ashley raced into the room. While he took in the fury in her eyes, a part of his brain acknowledged that she burst into his life on a regular basis. She was fearless, which he admired. Hers was real courage—she was brave even when she had something to lose.

She slammed the door behind her. "What the hell were you thinking?"

Her rage was a tangible life force in the room with him. Jeff turned away from his computer so that he could face her. Even as he wondered what she was talking about, he realized she'd never visited him at work before.

"Ashley, what seems to be the problem?"

Her eyes flashed with fire. "Don't give me that. Don't pretend you don't know. What was it, Jeff? A game? Did you think it was funny? How dare you play with my life! Were you even thinking? Didn't you care that I had goals and a plan? Damn you."

He didn't know what was wrong. He rose and walked around the desk so that he was standing in front of her. Had she finally figured out that his dreams weren't strange images from his subconscious, but were, in fact, the truth? Had she realized he wasn't like other men?

Tears filled her eyes. She angrily brushed them away. "Say something."

"I still don't know what's wrong."

Her mouth thinned. "How like a man. What am I supposed to tell Maggie? Did you even give her one thought in all of this?"

At the mention of her daughter's name, his heart froze. "Is something wrong with Maggie? Is she hurt?"

"She's fine. This has nothing to do with Maggie." She shoved him away from her. "You and your big sob story. To think I bought into it. I'm such an idiot. You lied to me. How could you?"

"Ashley?"

She glared at him. "I'm pregnant."

Chapter Fourteen

Ashley continued to talk but Jeff wasn't listening. He couldn't believe what she's said.

Pregnant?

He tried to figure out what, if anything, he was feeling, but he couldn't tell. It was as if his entire brain had shut down. Pregnant. He turned the word over and over in his mind wondering how it could be possible.

"And don't for a moment think that you're going to say something stupid like 'Who's the father?'" she said, still glaring at him. "You know exactly where I've been spending my nights. This baby is yours."

A baby. That was more real than hearing her say she was pregnant. Had they really produced a child together? A living being growing inside of her that would become an infant and grow into a child.

He hadn't thought he was human enough to father a child. He remembered what the doctor had talked about when there had been problems with Nicole. That he, Jeff, had a low sperm count. Something about less than optimal numbers. That it was unlikely he could father a child in the traditional manner, although there had been other alternatives if they'd been interested. By then, Nicole wasn't interested. She'd said that the reason he couldn't father a child wasn't about his sperm count but the fact that he was no longer human.

She'd been wrong.

Jeff had never thought to question the doctor further. Until Ashley had entered his life, he'd used condoms for health reasons. Although with her that had never seemed necessary. He knew he was healthy, so he hadn't worried about passing anything on to her. But he'd never considered that he might be able to get her pregnant.

"Are you even listening to me?" she demanded.

Something bright and alive flashed inside of him. It was hot and pure and it took him several seconds to recognize the feeling.

Joy. Pure, wonderful joy.

He grabbed her at the waist and swung her around the room. She shrieked and hung on to his shoulders.

"Jeff! Put me down. I'm not happy about this."

He knew, but he couldn't help smiling at her. "We're having a baby."

"I believe I was the one who informed *you* of that. Stop grinning like a sheep. This isn't good news."

He tried to sober. "I know. I'm sorry. I wasn't playing with you, Ashley. I didn't know I could get you pregnant. Based on what the doctor had told me before, I never thought it would be an issue. I really do have a low sperm count. If you would like the name and phone number of the doctor, I'll give it to you. I wasn't being irresponsible on purpose.''

She pulled away from him and moved over to the leather sofa by the back wall. Once there, she sank onto a cushion and dropped her head into her hands.

"I know,'' she said softly. "I never thought you planned this. I mean I know I sort of implied it by what I said, but that was more shock and temper than anything else.'' She raised her head and looked at him. "You might not have many sperm but the ones you have seem frisky enough.''

She drew in a shaky breath, then swore and started to cry. "I can't believe this is happening to me. I thought I finally had my life all together. I had so many plans for Maggie and myself and now I'm going to have a b-baby.''

The last word broke on a sob. Jeff knelt beside her. As he had before when she'd cried, he touched her tears, marveling in her ability to feel so much. To let herself live in the world rather than outside of it.

"I know you're confused and upset,'' he said soothingly. He was neither. The path was obvious to him. He'd created this problem in her life and he was going to fix it. "You don't have to be. Your plans will be different now, but that's not necessarily a bad thing. I'll be providing for you, Maggie and the baby. You can finish your degree or not. It's your choice.''

She blinked and several more tears ran down her cheeks. "That's crazy, Jeff. We're not your responsibility. Well, maybe the baby is, but not the rest of it.''

''I want the responsibility. I want to take care of you. I want you to marry me.''

Married? *Married!* Ashley stared at Jeff, unable to form any more words in her brain. Married?

''You want to marry me?'' she asked, not able to believe what he'd said.

''Yes. As soon as possible.''

She shook her head. When she'd first suspected the truth, she'd dismissed the possibility of being pregnant. Never one for a regular period, the length of time since her last one hadn't been much of a concern. But as the days had turned into weeks, she'd begun to wonder. Then yesterday when she'd stopped at the drugstore to buy vitamins for Maggie, she'd found herself in the family-planning aisle, studying the different pregnancy kits. Even as she'd told herself it wasn't possible, she'd bought one. Two hours ago, she'd had her hunch confirmed.

She'd been so angry, first at Jeff for what she'd thought were his lies, but mostly at herself. She knew better. She was smart and responsible. So why had she gotten so careless with something as important as birth control? She'd always wanted more kids, but not like this.

''You don't have to do this,'' she told him. ''While I'd appreciate some help until I get my degree, marriage isn't necessary.''

She wished he wouldn't talk about it anymore. She didn't want to be married to someone who didn't care about her. She didn't want to be an obligation.

He cupped her face in his large, strong hand. Despite not knowing how she was going to put her life back together, she couldn't help rubbing her cheek against his palm. If she had to have an unexpected pregnancy, she would prefer Jeff to be the father. At least she knew she was getting a very strong, intelligent gene pool.

"I want to marry you," he said, gazing into her eyes. "Not because it's the right thing to do, but because I don't want to let you go. I'm not willing to lose you, Maggie or the baby."

Happiness crashed over her like a wave. She flung her arms around him and pulled him close.

"You care!" she said, starting to cry all over again, but this time they were tears of happiness. "Oh, Jeff, I'd hoped you did, but I wasn't sure. You never said anything. You could be distant. I was afraid you were just in it for the sex."

She sniffed and straightened, then kissed him on the mouth, on his nose, on his cheeks, before hugging him again.

"I love you," she whispered fiercely. "I have for a long time. At least it's been coming on for a while. I knew for sure that weekend we went away. My very own warrior."

"Ashley."

He was the one to pull back this time. He wiped away her tears.

"You don't have to say this. I want to marry you."

"No. It's not because of the baby." She grasped his hands in hers. "Please don't think it's because of that or gratitude. I really mean it. I love you so much. You're everything I've ever wanted. I can't believe I got so lucky to find someone like you. Someone so good and strong. You're different from any man I've ever known.''

She sniffed, then smiled. ''I know the whole emotional thing is really hard for you, so I'm doubly honored that you would trust me with your heart. I swear, I'll never give you a reason to regret this. I'll love you forever.''

He leaned forward and kissed her. ''You make me very happy,'' he told her.

''And I'm even a pretty decent evasive driver,'' she teased, then kissed him back.

All her dreams were finally coming true, she thought as he pulled her close and hugged her. Jeff loved her more than anyone in the world. In his arms she could feel safe, loved and at home.

''Mommy, you have a secret,'' Maggie complained that night at dinner. ''I can tell.''

Jeff wasn't surprised the little girl had figured out something was different with her mother. Ashley practically glowed. Her smile was radiant, her step extrabouncy, her conversation excited.

''A secret?'' Ashley said, her voice teasing. ''You think so?'' She turned to smile at him, a smile full of adoration. ''What do *you* think, Jeff? Is there a secret?''

He knew she was playing a game and wanted him to be a part of it. But he couldn't be as lighthearted about the situation. He was confused and felt guilty. Which didn't make sense because he'd been telling the truth when he'd said he would marry her. He *wanted* to marry her. However, she thought he loved her.

Love. Jeff didn't know what the word meant. Not anymore. Perhaps there had been a time when he'd been a part of a family, just like everyone else. Those long-ago memories didn't have any place in his current reality. So when she said she loved him, he wasn't sure if he understood what that meant.

He believed in Ashley's capacity to love. He'd seen it firsthand with Maggie. Ashley was patient and caring. She'd seen him at his worst and she was still here. Wanting to be with him. Claiming to love him.

"Mommy, tell me!" Maggie pursed her lips together in a scowl. "I want to know!"

Ashley pulled her daughter onto her lap and hugged her. "Okay. It's a really good secret. I think you're going to be very happy."

Maggie's blue eyes widened. "Are we getting a kitten?"

"No. It's better than that."

Now that Ashley had Maggie's attention, she hesitated. Jeff knew her well enough to know that she was searching for the right words. She wanted to explain the situation simply and in a way that left the four-year-old feeling safe.

He was glad he wasn't the one who had to figure the best way to say it. Words had never been his strong suit. Actions had always been easier.

As Ashley started talking about how nice it had been to live in "Uncle Jeff's" house, he studied them. The overhead kitchen light illuminated their faces, making the similarities between them easy to spot. How much would their child look like Ashley? Or would the child look like him?

The questions startled him, reminding him again of

the fact that he and Ashley were going to have a baby together. He dropped his gaze to her flat stomach. A baby grew in there. He was still stunned that he'd been able to get her pregnant. Now that she and Maggie were going to be a permanent part of his world, he was determined to take care of them.

"Well," Ashley was saying, "what if we never had to leave Uncle Jeff's house? What if we lived here for always?"

Maggie looked at him, her rosebud mouth parting. "We can stay? Promise?"

His throat tightened. The sensation was unfamiliar. "I'd like that."

Ashley tucked a curl behind her daughter's ear. "Maggie, I love you very much. I will always love you."

"I know, Mommy. I love you, too."

"I also love Jeff. And he loves us. I'm going to marry him."

Jeff waited, his throat tight, his heart seemingly still. He and Ashley had discussed waiting to tell Maggie about the baby. She would need time to get used to her new family before having to adjust to having a younger sibling.

Maggie looked at him. "Will you be my daddy when you and Mommy get married?"

Odd feelings crashed through him. He couldn't identify any of them so he didn't know what they meant. However, they made it tough to talk. He had to swallow a couple of times before he could get out the words.

"Would you like that?"

She threw herself at him. "When we went to

church on Easter I asked God to send me a new daddy, and he did!''

Her small arms wrapped tightly around his neck. Her weight settled on his body. He hugged her back. With a fierceness that surprised him, he vowed to himself he would always keep this precious child safe. If that wasn't love, it was the best he could do.

''So you're okay with this?'' Ashley asked. ''You're happy that I'm marrying Jeff?''

''Daddy,'' Maggie said, planting a sticky kiss on his cheek. ''You're marrying Daddy.''

Tears filled Ashley's eyes. She wrapped her arms around them both. For the first time in many years, Jeff felt as if he was a part of something important and special. Daddy. The word felt both odd and right.

He shifted so he could reach his suit jacket, hanging behind him on the chair back. In the right outside pocket was a small box. He'd stopped to pick it up on his way home. Now he grabbed the box and held it out to Ashley.

Both females stared at the square of dark blue velvet.

''What is it?'' Ashley asked.

''What do you think?''

She shrugged, then lightly touched the top of the box. ''Maybe an engagement ring?''

''Got it in one.''

He was suddenly nervous. Should he have waited and asked her if it was all right to buy her a ring? Should he have taken her shopping with him? He'd actually just stopped to look when he'd seen the elegant design and had known right away that it was perfect for her.

"Open it," he told her.

She took the box and did as he requested. Both Ashley and Maggie gasped as she drew out an emerald-cut diamond on a platinum band. Smaller baguette-cut diamonds were set into the band. Light caught the larger gem and made it glow.

"It's gorgeous," Ashley breathed.

"Do you really like it?"

She looked stunned for another second or two, then threw her arms around his neck and hugged him close. "Jeff, it's so beautiful and way too expensive. You didn't have to do this for me."

"I wanted to."

"Thank you. You've made me very happy."

Her scent, the feel of her body, the pressure of her mouth on his were all familiar. They filled him with a confidence that he'd never felt before. In that moment he knew he could take on the world and win.

"Oh, Jeff."

Ashley snuggled against him in his bed. She curled herself around him, resting her head on his shoulder and gazing up at her engagement ring.

"I still think you spent way too much money."

"I don't, and it's my money. At least until we get married."

She turned and looked at him. "No. It will always be *your* money. I want you to keep everything you made before the marriage separate. That way it's not community property."

He frowned. "Why would you want that?"

"Because I'm not marrying you for your money. I love you. But if I start asking for things or taking what's yours, you'll start to question me, and I don't want that. Everything has happened so fast. Your last experience with marriage wasn't exactly positive. I want this to be different. I want it to be forever. So I need you to trust me.''

He smoothed her hair off her face. ''I trust you with my life,'' he said. Didn't she know that trusting or not trusting wasn't the problem?

''Good. Then keep everything you have now in your own name and it will never be an issue between us. Besides, in a couple of years I'm going to be the one making the big bucks, and then you'll be worried about *me* thinking *you're* in it for the money.''

She grinned and he couldn't help smiling in return. What twist of fate had brought this beautiful, giving woman into his life? How had he gotten so lucky as to have won her heart and that of her daughter?

''Speaking of my career, or the training thereof, I have finals in a couple of weeks.'' She rested her hand on his chest and her chin on her hand. ''I have to really buckle down and study, so I was thinking we could get married after that. Or did you want to wait longer?''

''I will marry you whenever you say,'' he told her. ''After finals works for me. What do you want to do?''

She wrinkled her nose. ''Something small is fine with me. Maybe just a couple of friends with a justice of the peace and then we all go out to dinner?''

''What about a honeymoon?''

She arched her eyebrows. ''What did you have in mind?''

''A couple of nights somewhere by ourselves.

Maybe San Francisco. Then a week or so with Maggie.''

She sighed contently. ''This is why I want to marry you. You're such a great man, Jeff. Thoughtful and caring. It means a lot to me that you're willing to bring Maggie.''

''I wouldn't want to leave her behind.''

''I agree.'' She hesitated, then ran her free hand through the hair on his chest. ''Do you think we did the right thing, not telling her about the baby? I mean, there's plenty of time. I won't really be showing until I'm well into my fourth month.''

''The wedding is enough for her right now.''

''Okay. That's what I thought, too.'' She looked at him. ''What about your family? Do you want to tell them about us? You've never said very much about them. Are you seriously estranged?''

His family? He hadn't thought about them over the past few years. ''No one got angry and stalked out,'' he said, ''if that's what you're asking. My visits made my folks uncomfortable so I stopped going.''

''Why?''

''For the same reason Nicole divorced me. I was different.''

''I bet they'd like to see you now,'' she told him. ''It's been a long time and I'm sure they miss you. Maybe you could give them a second chance.''

He shrugged. He didn't have an opinion one way or the other.

''You're their son,'' she persisted. ''You matter. They love you.''

''Do they?'' he asked, because he wasn't sure.

"What does that mean? What do you feel when you say you love me? How can you be sure?"

She laughed and rolled onto her back. "I'm sure because it's written in the stars. Because I hear the sound of the ocean when we're together, not to mention a choir of angels."

"No. Seriously. What do you feel? How do you know?"

She sat up, leaning against the headboard and pulled the covers up over her bare breasts. Her humor faded and her eyes darkened. "You're not joking? You really want to know what I feel when I say I love you?"

He nodded.

"Jeff?" She paused and licked her lips. "Why are you asking me that?"

Her voice sounded very small. He could see her pulse beating in her throat. As she watched him her heart rate increased and her skin paled.

He knew then that he'd made a huge mistake pursuing that line of questioning. He wished he could call back the words and talk about something else.

"You don't love me," Ashley breathed. Her hands tightened around the covers she held in front of herself. "Dear God, why didn't I see it before? You don't love me. You want to marry me because of the baby."

"No," he said quickly, even though it was true. "I care about you and Maggie very much. You're both important to me. More important than anyone has been in a long time. Maybe ever. I want to keep you both close and take care of you. I want to be there for you, your daughter and our child. I want to learn to be a good husband and father.''

Tears filled her hazel eyes. ''But you don't love us.''

Deep inside of him something began to ache. He knew that if he told her the truth, he risked losing her. But he couldn't lie.

''I don't know how. I don't know what love is. I feel something,'' he said, touching his chest. ''I want you. I miss you when we're apart. I want the best for you, Maggie and the baby. Is that love?''

Ashley felt the tears on her cheek. She told herself to say something, to scream, to run, but she was immobilized by disbelief and shock. All her life she'd wanted only one thing—to be loved by someone who would love her more than anything else in the world. Foolishly she'd given her heart to Jeff even knowing that he wasn't likely to care about her that way. When he'd proposed, she'd allowed herself to believe that he was more than she'd imagined.

She thought she'd finally found everything she'd ever wanted in the world, but she'd been wrong. It was all just an illusion.

''I can't,'' she murmured, not sure what she was saying she couldn't do. Stay? Marry him? Keep breathing?

Feeling returned to her limbs—a tingling pain as if they'd been asleep for a long time. She forced herself to climb out of bed and reach for her robe. Her body ached and it was difficult for her to walk.

''Ashley, where are you going?''

''To my room. I have to think.'' She had to figure out how everything had gone so terribly wrong.

* * *

Jeff lay in the darkness, listening to the silence in the house. Ashley had left him several hours before. While he knew what had gone wrong, he didn't know how to fix the situation. Was he supposed to go after her? Should he try to explain? Except what was there to say?

She wanted a piece of his heart. He'd figured out that much. He would have offered all of it, had it been his to give. But that tender organ had long since died, leaving him only a hollow shell of a man. There had been no other way to survive the horrors of what he'd seen and experienced. He'd ruthlessly cut out any delicate feelings because they were dangerous. He'd had to become a machine to survive. Now he was in a situation that required him to be a tender man and he no longer remembered how.

He rose and walked to the window. The night sky was surprisingly clear. He studied the stars as if the answers could be found there. Cold seeped in through the glass. He shivered.

Suddenly the coldness came from within. It was thick and dark and froze him to the center of his being.

She would leave him now.

Jeff leaned his forehead against the cool glass and held in the cry of anguish. No, he thought. She couldn't go. If she left, he would not survive. He could not. Without her he would turn into the robot of his nightmares. Without her he wouldn't have a chance.

Hurrying, he left his room and found his way to hers. The light was off, but she wasn't asleep. He could hear the soft sound of her weeping. Without saying anything, he climbed into her bed and pulled her close. She came to him willingly, holding him tight, pressing her cheek against his chest.

"Stay," she whispered.

"I will. Just don't leave me."

He breathed in the scent of her, the heat of her, needing her to chase away the chill. But the ice lingered, fueled by her tears and his knowledge that nothing had been resolved.

Chapter Fifteen

Three days later Ashley was just as hurt and confused as she'd been when she first realized that Jeff didn't love her. What was she supposed to do? Stay with him? Marry him anyway, knowing that he didn't love her? They were going to have a child together, which meant something to her. She thought it meant something to him. And Maggie adored him.

She pushed aside her accounting theory textbook and rose to her feet. With all the emotional conflict in her life, she was having a difficult time studying. Maybe a break would help.

She went in search of Jeff and Maggie. He'd offered to take care of her daughter for the evening, giving Ashley time to study. She'd appreciated the offer and had accepted. Not only so she could hit the books, but because she found it difficult to be with

Jeff these days. She kept trying to figure out what he was thinking and feeling.

As far as she was concerned, the formula was simple. If he didn't love her, she wasn't staying. They could work out some kind of arrangement for their child later, but she wouldn't be married to a man who didn't love her. So why was she still here? What was she waiting for? Was it inertia, or something more? Was she stalling for time because she was hoping for a miracle, or did she really believe that Jeff's feelings were deeper than he realized?

Ironically, while her life before Jeff had been more difficult financially, in other ways it had been a whole lot easier. Her choices had been simple. Now she found herself deciding one minute to stay because she couldn't imagine life without Jeff, then the next minute, telling herself they would leave in the morning.

She walked into the family room. Jeff and Maggie sat on the floor, her daughter on his lap, his back pressed against the sofa. They were watching a cartoon movie based on the Tarzan legend.

Maggie was draped across Jeff, her head leaning trustingly against his chest. One of his big hands rested on her belly and she absently tugged on his fingers. On the floor lay a half-dozen dolls in various stages of dress, surrounded by scattered clothes. Obviously they'd been playing one of Maggie's favorite games of pretend: Fashion Show.

Ashley couldn't help smiling as she imagined Jeff fumbling with the miniature fastenings of the small but intricate clothing. Yet she knew without having been in the room that he'd been patient with Maggie, following her lead and making her feel special. She knew that he would have little interest in the Tarzan movie, yet he would watch it as if it was a matter of world peace. That next week he would willingly watch it again.

She leaned against the doorframe and folded her arms over her chest. She wanted answers. Ashley shook her head. No. She wanted a sure thing. She wanted to know that Jeff was the one. As if there were only one perfect person. She didn't want to make a mistake; she didn't want another loser in her life.

She wanted him to promise that he would love her forever. And when he couldn't say the words, she wanted to leave him. But what about his actions? What about the fact that when it had really counted, he'd show up for both her and Maggie? What about every kind thing he'd done? What about how he'd taken her into his world, afraid it would drive her away, yet needing her to see the truth of what he did? What about him wanting to marry her because he'd made a baby with her?

He was, she realized, the most honorable man she'd ever known. How could she have doubted him?

Jeff might not know how to tell her how he felt but he *showed* her every day. And isn't that what mattered? Wasn't it all about actions rather than any slick words? He might not know the state of his heart, but with every kindness, every moment of caring and patience, he demonstrated what he felt.

"Ashley?"

She looked up and saw that he'd seen her. She read the questions in his eyes. Things hadn't been right since they'd had that late-night talk. She glanced at her daughter and knew this wasn't the time.

"I just wanted to say hi," she told him. "And tha
I love you."

Hope flared in his eyes. "Still? Even..." His voic
trailed off.

"Still," she assured him and felt contentment. H
was the one she wanted, for always.

After Maggie was in bed that night, she wen
searching for him. He was in his study, going ove
some papers. As she approached, he set down his pen

"We have to talk," he said.

"I know." She circled around the desk and slippe
onto his lap. Then she wrapped her arms around hi
neck and kissed him. "I've decided that we're goin;
to be all right. You need some time to come to grip
with all that's happened between us. It's been fast an
a real change. I understand that. You've spent th
past, what, fifteen years living like some Rambo guy
Family life is going to be an adjustment. I trust you
Completely."

"I'm glad," he said, setting her on her feet an
standing next to her. "Because we have to go over
few things before I leave."

"Leave?"

"My trip to the Mediterranean. The Kirkma
case."

"Oh. Yeah. You told me." In all the emotiona
trauma, she'd forgotten. She followed him over to th
leather sofa and settled next to him. She pointed t
the folder waiting on the coffee table. "State se
crets?"

"No."

"A security plan?"

"Not exactly."

She tilted her head. "Okay. You're not being wildly chatty. Why don't you take over the conversation."

"I want to talk about my will." He opened the folder and drew out a thick document. "I saw my lawyer yesterday to get a new will. I've left everything to you, except for two separate life insurance policies I had set up for Maggie and the baby. You're the trustee for both policies. It should be enough to cover raising them, along with college."

She stared at the document, but couldn't make it come into focus. A will? "I don't understand."

"If things don't go well, I want you to be taken care of. The business is set up with an automatic sale of my half to Zane, if something happens to me, and the same if he dies. You'll receive the proceeds from the sale, along with the house. I have a 401k, investments, checking and savings accounts. Brenda will get in touch with my financial adviser if anything happens, and Jerry can walk you through it all."

"No." She pushed the folder away. "I don't want to talk about this. Not now. I told you. I'm not interested in your money."

His gray gaze was steady. "I understand that, Ashley, and I believe you. However, if I don't come back, I want you taken care of."

If I don't come back.

She slid into the corner of the sofa. "Don't come back? What are you talking about?"

He sighed. "Probably nothing. This isn't an extremely high-risk operation."

Operation? "Are we talking about your business trip?"

"It's a security detail. These men are very highly placed. There have been both death and kidnapping threats. We've prepared for the worst and I'm sure everything will be fine. But if something happens, I want you to have financial security."

She sprang to her feet. "No. I don't want financial security. I want you to come back."

"I'm sure I will."

She pointed to the folder. "You're *not* sure. That's why we're having this conversation. Jeff, are you telling me that you could die on this trip?"

He shifted uncomfortably on the sofa. "It's unlikely."

"How unlikely?"

"Less than a thirty percent chance."

Her mouth dropped open. Thirty percent? There was a thirty percent chance he could die? While he was gone?

"No," she said firmly. "No. You can't go. You cannot die. Not until we're both old. I don't want you to die." She'd just found him. She refused to lose him.

"Ashley, be reasonable. This is what I do."

"You're crazy, then. How can you walk out on Maggie and me? And what about the baby?" She paced to his desk, then spun to face him. "You can't. You just can't. Dammit, Jeff, you're not some solitary soldier giving his all for God and country. This is just some assignment. You can't leave like this. It's wrong. You have a responsibility to us. We need you to come home to us."

"This is what I do."

"No, it isn't. You run a security company. You have a staff. You have other people to do this kind of thing."

"So I should send someone else out there to die?"

She felt as if he'd hit her in the stomach. She clutched her midsection and bent at the waist.

He was going to die. That's what he was trying to tell her. The claim of it only being a thirty percent chance had been a lie designed to calm her fears.

"Ashley—"

"No!" she shouted, straightening and glaring at him. "All my life the people I've cared about and loved haven't loved me back. Not enough to stay. Not enough to keep from dying. I thought you were different. I thought you really cared, but because of your background you couldn't get in touch with your feelings. But now I know that I was wrong. You can't express your feelings because you don't have them. I thought you would change and realize you love us, but you won't. You don't love us. You're going to leave me and die, just like everyone else. You don't think I'm worth living for."

He rose. "You're wrong. You are worth living for. I have every intention of coming back to you."

"That's not good enough. I don't want you to go."

"I have to go. It's my job." He hesitated. "You knew what I was before, Ashley. Nothing has changed."

"Yes, it has." Before, she hadn't realized the truth. "Loving someone means wanting to stick around."

As soon as she said the words, she braced herself for him to say he didn't love her at all, so what did staying matter. But he didn't. Instead his expression turned sad.

"I would have thought loving someone meant accepting every part of that person," he said. "You knew who and what I was when you first met me, so I don't understand why it's suddenly a problem. It's ironic. Nicole could accept what I did, but not what I'd become. You understand who I am, yet you won't accept what I do. I guess we both expected more of each other."

Ashley felt as if he'd slapped her. She'd been so sure she was the one in the right and that he was wrong. But his words caught her off guard. Too stunned to speak, she could only watch as he walked out of the room.

Jeff waited the entire night, but she never came to him. He'd tried to go to her, but her door had remained closed and she hadn't answered his light knock.

The next morning he packed his suitcase and made his way downstairs. He'd left the folder on the coffee table in his study. If something happened to him, he wanted Ashley to be able to find it.

She was in the kitchen with Maggie. The dark circles under her eyes told him that she, too, had had a restless night. As they stared at each other, he wished he could find the words to make it right between them. He wished there was a way to explain why he had to do this job—why he had to do every job. That stepping into the line of fire was the only way to atone.

Maggie saw him and scrambled out of her seat.

"Daddy, Daddy, Mommy says you have to go away and I don't want you to go."

She flung herself at him. With an ease he wouldn't have believed possible just a couple of months ago, he set down his suitcase, bent low and picked her up, swinging her into his arms. She clung to him.

"Don't go," she said, her big blue eyes filled with tears.

"I have to. This is about work. But I'll be home in about a week."

"A week is a very long time."

"I know. I'll miss you."

As he spoke he looked over her head toward Ashley, but the woman who had so changed him wouldn't meet his gaze. She sat at the table, carefully stirring her coffee.

Maggie rested her head on his shoulder and sighed. She was so small, he thought uneasily. How could she possibly survive? He found himself wanting to stay, to make sure that she was going to be all right. But he couldn't. He had a job to do.

"I'll bring you something," he told her as he set her on the floor.

She brightened immediately. "A kitten?"

"No. Mommy and I have to talk about that first. But something nice."

"Something for Mommy, too?"

He looked at Ashley. She was still staring intently at her coffee. "Yes, something for Mommy."

Jeff hesitated. He wanted to say something that would make things better between them. He wanted to heal the breach, but he didn't know how. In the end all he did was pick up his suitcase.

"I need to get to work. I'll guess I'll see you in a week."

"Will you call?" Ashley asked without looking up

Phone her? He'd never considered the possibility But he could. Staying in touch would be easy.

"Sure." He calculated the time difference. "Say the early evening, after dinner?"

She nodded. "That would be nice. Thank you."

He wanted to go to her and pull her to her feet and into his arms. He wanted to beg her to tell him that she wouldn't give up on him, that it wasn't over between them. He wanted to know how he was supposed to make her happy when everything about their relationship confused him.

Instead he said nothing. He turned on his heel and walked out of the kitchen. Maggie called after him.

"Mommy and I love you."

He could only hope it was still true.

Six hours later he pored over the diagrams of the villa one last time. The private jet would take off from Boeing Field at four. The team was already assembled, the equipment checked.

"I can't believe you're doing this," Zane said as he walked into Jeff's office.

"What are you talking about?" he asked his partner.

Zane stalked over to the table and stabbed at the papers. "I can't believe you're really going to do this."

"The job? It's my responsibility."

"No. It's *our* responsibility. I'm a partner in this remember. I can do this job." Zane glared at him. "

was bad enough when you wanted all the glory for yourself, but now you have a family to think about.''

Glory? "Is that what you think?" Jeff asked. "That taking the most dangerous assignments is about glory? I never wanted my name in the papers. None of that mattered.''

Zane's dark eyes were bleak when he spoke. "If it's about the dead, don't you think I have some ghosts of my own? Just because I was a sharpshooter doesn't mean I wasn't involved. Killing from a distance is still killing, Jeff. When I had to plan operations, the numbers of the dead weren't faceless. I studied the recon photos afterward to see how my plan had been carried out. I could see what I'd done in every shade of color.''

Jeff stared at his partner. "I hadn't realized," he said.

Zane shrugged. "Before, it wasn't important for you to know, but things are different. You have Ashley and Maggie now.''

And the baby, but Zane didn't know about that yet. A family. That's what his partner was saying. Jeff had responsibilities for more than the job. At one time he would have agreed, but not now. Ashley might claim to love him, but he doubted it was true. She loved parts of him. The parts she could admire. But the true blackness of his soul was beyond her. He thought she understood who and what he was, but he'd been wrong. She was already pulling away.

What he couldn't admit to Zane, what he could barely think to himself, was how much it hurt. He'd allowed himself to believe. When she'd heard about his nightmares and hadn't turned away, he'd experienced his first spark of hope. Later, instead of being frightened off by the executive retreat, she'd had fun. He'd told her more details about his past and still she'd stayed, eventually claiming to love him. And he'd believed her because he'd been desperate to keep her in his life.

But in the end, she couldn't handle what he did. She wanted him to change, to take a job that wouldn't put him in danger. She wasn't willing to love all of him.

"I don't think Ashley and Maggie are going to be sticking around much longer," Jeff said, gathering up the diagrams. "Ashley doesn't approve of these kind of missions."

"Can you blame her? Who wants to see someone she loves facing down a bullet?"

"It's what I do."

"That's complete bull and you know it. You chose how you participate in the assignment. You hire the best and train them to be better, then instead of letting them get on with their job, you meddle." Zane took a step closer to him. "You know what I think, Jeff? I think you're afraid. You care about Ashley and her daughter and that scares you. You've never had to care before. Suddenly, after all these years, you have something to lose. What if your edge is gone? What if at the last minute you don't want to take the bullet? But instead of celebrating the fact that you have a chance at a normal life, you walk away."

Zane glared at him in disgust. "You're an idiot. Don't you get it? Chances like this don't come along very often."

"You don't have anyone in *your* life," Jeff said, trying to ignore the truth of his friend's words.

"You're right. Because the one person I was supposed to be with died. There's not a single day that goes by without me thinking about her, wishing things could be different. I lost my chance. What's your excuse?"

Jeff wasn't sure what to say. "I'm sorry," he mumbled. "I didn't know."

"Yeah, well, now you do. So quit being a jerk who would rather take a bullet in the back than admit he might have fallen in love."

Ashley couldn't get Jeff's words out of her head. She kept telling herself that he was wrong, that she hadn't betrayed him. She was the injured party. But no matter how many times she told herself that, she couldn't quite make herself believe it.

She paced the length of the kitchen, ignoring her open accounting books. While she knew she should be studying, she couldn't stop thinking about Jeff. Thinking and watching the clock. His plane would take off in less than two hours. After that she wouldn't see him for a week…or maybe not ever again.

"I can't go through this," she said, squeezing her eyes shut. "I can't sit around waiting for him to die. All I wanted was someone to love me back. To want to live for me and love me more than anyone. An unconditional love."

She opened her eyes and stared unseeingly out the window. Jeff was never going to love her that way.

She wanted to scream her frustration. She wanted

to throw something. She knew in her heart she wasn't as angry about his work as she was about the loss of her dream. She'd thought they would have a chance, but she'd been wrong. Damn the man for not loving her on her timetable and in the way she'd always imagined. Didn't he know he was messing with her lifelong dream? Ever since her sister had died, she'd ached to feel safe again. But with Jeff running off to throw himself in front of a bullet, she could never feel that way.

She could never—

Ashley froze in the center of the kitchen. She blinked once, then again. She wanted Jeff to love her on her timetable. She wanted him to love her unconditionally. *She* wanted.

But what about Jeff? Didn't he deserve the same wants and desires? Wasn't he entitled to a love that encompassed all of him, not just the parts she really liked? Who was she to dictate his life? As he'd pointed out the previous night, she'd known what he was when she'd met him. So why was she so angry about it now? Was it possible that she wanted to be loved unconditionally without doing the same in return?

As if showing a movie, her brain flashed pictures of her time with Jeff. From the first moment they'd met, he'd been giving, gentle and kind. He didn't know how to be a husband or a father, yet he was willing to take on both jobs. The second she'd told him about the baby, he'd wanted to marry her. In the past couple of months, he'd started to change, opening up more, feeling more. Perhaps he didn't know what was in his heart; perhaps he could never say the

words. But she knew. He was a man deeply commit-
ted. He was a man in love.

How could she have been so incredibly stupid?
Was she really going to let him walk out of her life,
possibly get killed, thinking she was mad at him? He
was everything she'd ever wanted. Why on earth was
she willing to let him go?

She glanced at the clock and panicked. There
wasn't much time.

"Maggie?" she yelled, running toward the family
room. "We have to go out right now. I want us to
say goodbye to Jeff."

Jeff crossed to the waiting area. The jet was due to
take off in about ten minutes. His team was in place.
They'd finished their last equipment check and were
getting ready to board when he heard a high-pitched
voice.

"Daddy! We want to say goodbye."

Stunned, Jeff turned slowly and saw Maggie and
Ashley waving from the entrance to the building. The
little girl broke away from her mother and ran toward
him. She held out her arms and threw herself at him.

"Mommy drove really fast," Maggie confided before giving him a wet kiss on his cheek. "We didn't
want to miss you."

He looked at Ashley for confirmation. She
shrugged sheepishly. "I wasn't reckless and I didn't
go over the speed limit—much."

A smile tugged at the corners of her mouth. She
wore jeans and a sweater and she was the most beautiful woman he'd ever seen.

''You're not mad at me anymore?'' he asked, not sure what could have changed her mind.

She moved close and joined her daughter in wrapping her arms around him. ''I'm sorry, Jeff. I shouldn't have said all those things.'' She looked up at him and grinned. ''Just because you're an idiot doesn't mean I'm going to stop loving you.''

Her words were like a soothing balm on the open wounds of his heart.

''Besides,'' she said. ''You have to come back and marry me. Maggie wants you to be her dad. I want you to be my husband and we have that other consideration.''

He knew she was referring to the baby. He put Maggie on the ground and took Ashley's hands in his. ''But this is what I am. I'm not going to change. I'm a soldier, Ashley. Parts of me will never see the light of day.''

''I know. While that doesn't make me happy, I accept and love all of you. Just don't you dare die out there. I'll be so angry, I'll hunt you down in the afterworld.''

''Are you sure?''

She nodded. ''I understand why you have to question me, Jeff. I'm sorry for how I acted. You're the best man I've ever known. It's okay that you can't speak from your heart yet. I even get that you may never be able to say the words. But your actions have a voice of their own and they tell me how you feel.''

She hesitated, then shrugged. ''All my life I've wanted someone to love me more than anything. I finally figured out I'd better be worth that kind of devotion. Which means I don't have the right to change your life. As you pointed out to me last night, I knew exactly who and what you were when I fell in love with you.''

She rose on her toes and kissed him on the mouth. "We'll miss you while you're gone and we'll be waiting for you to return. I love you.''

Jeff released her hands. Ashley watched him embrace her daughter, then he hugged her one last time. She tried not to cling to him, but it was hard. She wanted to beg him to stay. She wanted to plead her case one last time, telling him that they needed him alive. But she didn't. He had a job to do and she needed to respect that.

So she put on a brave face as he walked away and kept the tears at bay until he walked out of the hangar and toward the jet waiting on the runway. She saw Zane climbing the stairs. Jeff was right behind him. It was only then that she allowed herself to give in to the sadness filling her.

"Mommy, why are you crying?" Maggie asked.

"I'm going to miss Jeff very much."

Tears spilled out of her daughter's eyes. "Me, too. I'm going to pray for him every night.''

Ashley would do the same. Pray and wait and love him because he was the best part of her.

She picked up Maggie and held her close. Together they made their way to the car.

"We're a mess," Ashley said, trying to stem the flow of tears. "Look at us.''

She managed a feeble smile. Maggie attempted one, as well, but it wasn't very successful. Ashley fumbled with her keys. She set her daughter on the ground so she could push the metal into the lock.

Moisture blurred her vision. Behind them, the whine of the jet engine increased. He was leaving and she had to let him go.

She shoved the key into the lock, but it wouldn't fit. Then a warm, strong hand settled on top of hers, steadying her, guiding her, and the key slid home.

Ashley turned and saw Jeff standing behind her.

"How...? What...? Oh, thank you."

She flung herself into his arms, clinging as if she would never let go.

"Zane said I was an idiot for leaving you and Maggie," he murmured against her hair. "I finally figured out he was right. Besides, he always did hate sharing the glory."

She didn't know what to say. Happiness flooded her, filling her so much, she thought she might start to glow.

"You're really here? You're not leaving?"

He bent and picked up Maggie. "No more dangerous assignments," he promised. "I can't be fearless anymore. After all, I have something wonderful in my life now. Three somethings I don't want to lose."

"I can count to three," Maggie informed them. "Daddy, if you're not going away, can I have a kitten?"

"Absolutely."

Ashley laughed, then kissed Jeff. He held them both close.

"I get it," he said softly, staring into her eyes. "I finally understand what I've been fighting for so long. I know what's in my heart. It's why I couldn't leave.

I love you, Ashley. And Maggie and—'' he glanced at her stomach ''—you know.''

"Really?"

"More than anything in the world. For always. With you I can finally find my way home.''

Epilogue

The summer sun was warm and bright in the sky. Jeff looked up from the book he was reading as Maggie and her best friend, Julie, ran across the backyard. They were followed by two golden retrievers, sisters from the same litter. Laughter filled the air, making him smile.

He turned his attention to the shade in the corner where Ashley lay on a blanket, an eighteen-month-old blond boy snuggled at her side. As he watched the woman he loved and his firstborn son, he felt a familiar sensation of happiness and contentment. He could never have imagined his life turning out like this.

David Jeffrey Ritter had arrived exactly on schedule, claiming the attention of the entire family. Last May, Ashley had graduated with honors. She'd taken